CONVERSATIONS WITH LIKKA STO' RUFUS

Odie Hawkins aka Willie West

authorHOUSE®

AuthorHouse™
1663 Liberty Drive
Bloomington, IN 47403
www.authorhouse.com
Phone: 833-262-8899

Published by AuthorHouse   09/07/2021

ISBN: 978-1-6655-3715-5 (sc)
ISBN: 978-1-6655-3716-2 (e)

Library of Congress Control Number: 2021918037

Print information available on the last page.

Any people depicted in stock imagery provided by Getty Images are models,
and such images are being used for illustrative purposes only.
Certain stock imagery © Getty Images.

Front Cover by Carlos Spivey
https://www.carlosspiveyart.com/
and https://www.etsy.com/shop/CarlosSpiveyArt

Author's Photo and inserts by Zola Salena-Hawkins
www.flickr.com/photos/32886903@N02

Dedicated to Zola Salena-Hawkins aka "ZiZi,
The Kosmic Muffin, with Love and Respect
---Bright Moments

Table of Contents

Table Of Contents
- Photographs

CHAPTER 1

A couple weeks into June, Virus time, 2020. I had discovered the cool pleasure of mixing one shot of Seagram's gin with two shots of Jamaican ginger beer, poured over ice with a few mint leaves from the backyard spice rack. It was going to be another hot day and I wanted to get ready for it.

In addition to everything else, I had the new novel under my ballpoint. Yeahh, write, scribble it out first, Brother Willie, then type. That was/is my method, the way I work. A few of my friends thought it was weird that I wasn't more dependent on the latest technology and all that.

I didn't have a good counter argument for them, so I let it alone. What I could've said was this – "I have five published novels to my credit; how many do you have?" – But I let it alone. If you live long enough, and deal with enough people you should know when to hold and when to fold.

In any case, concerning my friends, they thought well enough of my work to nickname me – "The Undergroundmaster". So, they weren't being mean spirited when they asked me – "Say Willie, when are you gonna get behind that computer, pal? You would be able to write twice as many books as you have now."

I couldn't tell Randolph, one of my best friends that I wasn't anxious to write twice as many books, I wanted to write twice as well. Have to leave it there for the time being.

Off I go to my local liquor store in the shopping plaza place ten blocks south of me to cop this pint of Seagram's gin. Ten blocks away, almost a walkable distance in Long Beach, California. But who wants to walk anywhere in Southern California, unless you're in a hiking mood? I adjusted my mask, hopped in my VW and clutched away to the liquor store. Most of the people in my neighborhood had masked up early in the game. Seems that they didn't have to be reminded that wearing a mask and maintaining a "social distance" from your fellow being was the way to survive.

Parking my car and strolling toward the liquor store, I took notice of the usual "likka sto' gang", the quartet of men (and sometimes a woman) who hung out in front of the liquor store. Or a few yards to either side of the liquor store.

They were usually a bit boozed, or high from something or other. I felt for them in a way because they gave me the impression that they had nothing better to do than hang around the liquor store. We usually exchanged glances, never spoke to each other.

The Militant Pan Handler

It was easy to spot the latest member of the gang. Number one, he had taken a stance, a real social distance from the quartet who were having a fugal argument about something. A small, slender guy with a white face mask that said in black letters "I am Black History". I was struck by that. And by his posture. He wasn't slumped down, bent over as though the world had crushed him. I'm taking all of this in as I strolled toward the entrance of Mr. and Mrs. Kim's liquor store.

A small, slender guy, about 5'3-5, but with what somebody once called "Presence". Aside from the stance, there was his outfit, his costume, if you wanted to think about the way he was dressed. A white Halibut cap cocked at a rakish angle. A V-necked white T-shirt, neatly creased blue jeans (I could see that they were dirty and a pair of black sandals that were a couple sizes too large for his feet. And to round things off he had a male diddy bag slung over his right shoulder.

We looked into each other's eyes as I walked past him to go inside the liquor store. A character, if ever there was one. That's the first thought that struck me.

"Long time, no see." That was Mr. Kim's standard greeting to me. I think I had been just another customer until the day I asked him if he had Tsing Tao, a really fine Chinese beer.

"I know it, but I don't have. Maybe next time."

A week later I happened to be passing the liquor store and popped in. Mrs. Kim greeted me.

"Sir, we have."

I think it came from my seven brutal years climbing up the Hapkido-Tae Kwon Do ladder, this understanding of the Korean verbal shorthand. I went to their cold storage and there it was – four six packs of Tsing Tao. I copped two and asked ....

"How did you get the Tsing Tao?"

"My husband go to Filipino market in Norwalk for fish. They have it. He buy for you."

"Well, I really appreciate that. Tell him I said Kamsamnida."

This was way before the virus really hit, so I could see the expression in her eyes. She was totally stunned because I had said, "thank you" in Korean. A couple weeks later I was back on the scene.

"Long time no see." Mr. Kim greeted me with a smile in his eyes, something I hadn't seen before. He actually seemed pleased to see me.

"My wife says that you speak Korean."

"No, not really, only a few words ... bi bim bap, bulgokee, Hap ki do, Tae Kwon do."

"You know Hap Ki do – Tae Kwon do?"

3

"I have a red belt in Hap Ki do and the black belt in Tae Kwon do."
No bragging, just the truth."

"I have saved the Tsing Tao for you."

I thought that was very thoughtful of him, a nice thing to do. I
didn't have the heart to tell him that I had tripped to the Filipino market
and copped a six-pack the week after I found out where it was.

"Long time no see."

"Well, you know how it is, if you spend too much time in liquor
stores you could wind up like the people in front of your store."

I never made it seem like I was an anti–Korean liquor store owner,
or anything like that. I made it clear that he was a man doing bidness
and I was a customer. We both had a choice.

"I'll have a pint of Seagram's Gin."

Mr. Kim could cover a lot of ground while he reached over to his
liquor shelves. He surveyed the two young men who wandered into
the store; it seemed that his eye followed the dude who strolled to the
right as his right eye pinpointed the one who meandered to the left.
He was alert.

He took my twenty and gave me my Gin and change, all the while
hawking the two would be shoplifters.

"Have a nice day, Mr. Kim."

"Yes sir, you also."

The would-be shoplifters could see that they were under the gaze
of his radar eyes and slipped out of the door ahead of me.

"Brother Black History" was still in place. There was something
about the look he gave me over the top of his mask that drew me to
him. I strolled over to him, curling a dollar bill up in my right palm. I
felt that I had to give him something. Maybe it was because he looked
so proud, so distinctive.

He looked down at my outstretched hand, checked the bill and
shook hands with me. I was about to walk away from him when I was
halted by this deep, gravelly voice.

"So, what am I supposed to do with this, big shot?"

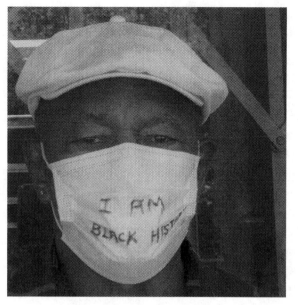

Melvin Montaigne Dixon, III
Aka "Likka Sto' Rufus"

The deep, gravelly voice coming out of this little guy was like hearing Redd Foxx again. I missed a step, got stalled would be a better description. I felt like I was being made to reply to a reasonable question. I turned and walked back to face "Brother Black History," from a safe distance, of course.

"I'm sorry, what was your question?"

"I didn't bite my tongue; I asked you – what am I supposed to do with this?" He held the curled-up dollar bill in his hand like it was something nasty. I wanted to answer his question, but I couldn't think of a decent answer. I stood there, trying to process the situation.

This guy was a panhandler, a beggar, if you wanted to get crude about it. And he was questioning my rationale for giving him a dollar. Only a dollar.

I couldn't figure out what to say to him, so I added a five-dollar bill to his one-dollar bill.

"There, how's that?"

"That's better," he gravel-growled at me. I felt the urge to go sarcastic on him.

"So, what're you going to do with all of your newfound wealth?"

I wasn't prepared to hear the serious tone in his gravelly voice.

"Well, it'll give me enough to get Tarzan...."

"Tarzan? Who is Tarzan?"

"Tarzan is my cat. It'll give me enough to get Tarzan a couple cans of good cat food, buy myself a lottery ticket. And a bag of organic figs, apples ... from Trader Joe's."

I think I wanted to hear – "a cold beer" – at the end of his recitation. But that was it. That was his answer to my sarcastic question. I felt like nipping his "I am Black History" mask off of his face, to take a look at the grinning face behind the mask. Or was he grinning? I decided to leave well enough alone.

I was opening my car door when one of the "likka sto' gang" staggered up to me. Uhh ooh, more stuff to deal with. I was about to tell her – "Sorry, sweetheart, I already gave at the office."

A full figured, middle aged woman, somebody's grandmother. She spoke in a soft soprano.

"Don't mind Likka Sto', baby, he been like that ever since he showed up."

"Why do you call him Likka Sto'?"

"Well, look yonder, you see that guy standin' over there, next to the drug sto'?"

"Yeah, I see him."

"Well, his gov'ment name is Rufus, but since he was handlin' the drug sto', people started callin' him Drug Sto' Rufus."

"Handlin'?"

"You know, askin' peoples for money."

"Oh ..."

"So, when this brother show up, handlin' in front of the Likka Sto', peoples started callin' him "Likka Sto' Rufus."

"What's his real name?"

She shrugged her shoulders and staggered back to the circle. It was the first time I had actually spoken with any bona fide member of the "likka sto' gang". I could've said that she was the second member, after "Likka Sto". But I had to put him in a different category, he wasn't one of the gang.

A message from ZiZi: "*Willie, I hope you're in a cool place, hydrating yourself regularly, doing all of the things that one has to do to survive in the desert. I can't be too sarcastic because, as you know, San Francisco is being baked too.*

This may not be the end of the world, but it almost feels like it. Enough of the maudlin shit. Are you coming up here this weekend? Or am I coming down there? And stop doing that salacious smile about "coming," you rascal you! I can e-mail/view you!

In any case, no matter what, I know it will be a delicious treat to be quarantined with you, no matter whether it's here or there. I know you're writing now, so I'm not going to belabor you with romantic ultimatums.

However, I would like an answer to my reasonable question before the end of the day. Today is Tuesday, as you already know. And tomorrow will be Wednesday if we survive all of the latter-day madness. The reason I'm talking about the weekend so soon?

Well, let's face it, the weekend is always staring us in the face, no matter what day it is. So let me know whether it's going to be here or there. I don't give a shit which city we're going to be in, we'll be together —

Love, Z"

Willie re-read the e-mail several times as he mixed his gin–ginger Jamaican beer–mint leaf libation over liberal mounds of ice. ZiZi Lago. He sprawled back in his writing chair. ZiZi Lago.

Big Harry's "*bait line*" was filled with promises…. "" *'ey you, Willie West, Undergroundmaster 'n all that shit. You better come on 'n go with me to this set, man.*

The rumor is that they gonna have about eight Sojourney Truths, six Oprahs, five Angelas, three or four Karen Basses and a heap of sexualized political people.

You don't wanna go?'"

I went and met ZiZi. I found her; a 4-feet 9-inch magnet, being drawn into her orbit by seasoned operatives of all political stripes, seasoned bullshitters, cynical exploiters, jive ass folks, a few honest minds.

I stood off to one side, listening to her dispense Dracular stuff to those who really wanted to know what the real deal was.

"Escochue y'all, I'm three lessons behind in my Spanish lessons, so bear with me. Please understand, all of you, all of those who really want to know what I think, and not what they think, I think. Got that? Here's my honest to God truth on this.

The man who is about to be USHERED out of the White House, an unfortunate name for a multi-racial/multi-colored nation, is giving us a chance to recognize, in real time, how a syphilitic sore/chancre survives the processes we've had in place for almost three hundred years –fuck all of the chicken shit stipulations that the Founding Fathers put into the original document.

Concern yourselves with the would-be-demon king asshole who is saying – Gimme! 'I'm saying – No!'"

That's a sample of what I heard when I went to this event. And shortly thereafter, I found us, me and ZiZi, walking on the ocean, holding hands, talking to each other, SERIOUSLY. My return e-mail was "I'm coming."

A gorgeous weekend in one of the most romantic cities in America, San Francisco. A beautiful time with my wife to be. We felt that it was only going to be a matter of months before the Big decision was made. Reality was forcing me, us, to lean toward San Francisco.

"Willie, look, I don't care where we live, to be frank with you. I just want us to be together; the snag is this – I'm one of the senior partners at Greenberg, Shafton and Jacobs. What it means is that I've managed to bust thru the glass ceiling that was made of White racism, sexism, nepotism and God only knows what else.

Our firm is based here, and it means a lot, as you know, to be at the base. You're a freelance writer, a wonderful writer I might add, and you can do your work anywhere in the world…"

Like I said, reality was forcing me to lean toward San Francisco. I really and truly loved San Francisco, with the lovely ambience. Even in the middle of the plague, with people all masked up and being forced to stay six feet away from each other, it was still a beautiful scene.

The thing I hated to confess to ZiZi is the fact that I was scared shitless of the hills. The first time I drove on Divisidero, going from point A to point D, I almost broke down and cried. I just couldn't believe that I was going to make it to Lombard.

As a matter of fact, I did make it. My brakes blanked out on me as I shot straight thru the Lombard/Divisidero intersection. If there was ever a time for me to pray, I prayed. And survived. But the experience left me a negative vibe about the 'Frisco hills."

$\text{\reflectbox{\textbf{W}}}$

Back on the level streets of Long Beach. Back to the outline for "The Latest Cult". The ideas to bake into the novel came slowly, but I felt I had to be patient and just allow the flow to happen. Finally, after four days of being patient, allowing the flow to happen and all that, I got into a semi-mellow groove that took me into ten pages about the state of politics in America.

I had read most of the books about Trump and his White House, feeling that they seemed to have left something out, something I felt I could supply. I couldn't put my finger on what it might be, this missing ingredient, so I decided to pay Mr. Kim's liquor store a visit. I had the ginger beer, all I needed was the gin.

CHAPTER 2

The Likka Sto' Fraternity

Well, I'll be damned! There he was, only a few feet to the left of where I last saw him, still standing at parade rest. I felt kind of anxious to talk with "Likka Sto" again. I should also mention that the "likka sto' gang" was still there, they had huddled under the shade of a large tree on the edge of the parking lot.

Five men and two women, animated, passing a large joint around clockwise, a bottle of cheap wine counterclockwise, maskless. I felt that same sense of sadness that I always felt when I saw Black people who had surrendered. O well …

"How's it goin', Rufus?"

He turned to give me a penetrating look over the top of his "I am Black History" mask.

"Do I know you?"

I felt like an idiot. I could definitely relate to where he was coming from. I was also one of those people who resented people who used your first name, no matter when they know you or not, no matter whether you wanted them to use your first name or not. It was simply a matter of respect. I don't know, maybe it kicked back to slavery, when all enslaved Africans were only accorded one name – "Hey you, Jupiter!"

"Uhh, my name is Willie West, I met you a couple weeks ago and I contributed six of my hard-earned dollars to your welfare."

"I hope you're not bitter or nothing, home."

I couldn't figure out what it was, the way he grabbed me, the way he said things. For the first time since I had put the mask on, and watched other reasonable people put their masks on, I felt like snatching my mask off and screaming at another human – "Awright! This is who I am. Now show me who you are."

But I didn't go there because Rufus chilled me out.

"Oh yeahh, Mr. Stingy Pants. I remember you."

"Long time, no see." Mr. Kim's standard greeting.

"Yeah, no see, long time." I think Rufus had aroused a bit of malice in me. Mr. Kim didn't seem to take any particular notice of my attempt to be funny. He served me my gin, gave me change for my twenty and waved me away with a sharp military salute. I strolled out asking myself ... wonder if Mr. Kim was in the army? Wonder what his story is?

These wondering thoughts took me out of the door.

"Oh, now that you've got your firewater, you're in a hurry to go home and get drunk, huh?"

His sarcastic, "Gravel Gerty" voice stopped me. What is it with this guy? What is it about him that butts me in the head? I turned and made a slow, deliberate stroll over to his position. That was the way I saw it. He had staked out a position.

I peeled a five spot out of my change to give to him. He accepted my "offering" as though I was paying him something that I owed him.

"This ain't going to mess up your budget for the rest of the week or anything, is it?"

"I hope not."

Truth be told, I felt like snatching my money back out of this dude's hand and saying something nasty. I resisted the urge and strolled back to my car. Weird, how the creative mind works. From giving him five dollars and strolling back to my car I came up with a hard thought. Who is this? Where is he coming from?

By the time I placed the gin in my glove compartment, I had organized a plan. I was going to find out who was conning me out of money. Well, actually he wasn't righteously conning me out of anything, I was conning myself.

"Back to make another contribution to the less fortunate?"

That was the way he welcomed me. I had to smile. This guy was something else.

"No, not another contribution today. You drink coffee?"

There was a slight pause before he answered – "Well, actually I'm a tea drinker."

"Awright, you don't drink coffee, you drink tea."

"O.k., you have tea, I'll have coffee. How 'bout having a cup of your favorite drink at the Salamat Po with me?"

The Salamat Po was this completely hip Filipino coffee house/bakery six business steps north of the liquor store. The mall was almost a village. The supermarket was the centerpiece flanged by the Salamat Po on the south, a nail shop, a laundromat and Mr. Kim's liquor store on the north side. And a couple restaurants that kept coming and going.

I say the Filipino place was hip because they had figured out how to do bidness in the middle of the plague. Number one, they were the first to extend their stuff out into the parking lot.

Here's the way they set it up: They had set up ten plastic covered cubicles as extensions of their business. They had placed ping pong type tables inside the cubicles, with seats six feet on each side of the tables, which were separated by plastic screen. It made the most squeamish feel safe. They could go inside this cubicle, take off their masks and talk across the ping pong table (thru the plastic curtain) and feel safe. That was the whole goal of the scene. Safety. No one wanted to risk getting the virus except Trump people.

"Yeahhh. I'll have a cup of tea with you at the Po, but I have to tell you, I am not into hugging and kissing men. Dig it?"

"Don't worry, pal, the last thing I would ask you is to hug and kiss me."

"Uhhh, you paying for this, right?"

"I'm paying."

"Let's go."

It only took a few steps to see that "Rufus" had a little hitch in his giddy up. He had a dip in his step that might've been mistaken for a hip way to walk, but I could see that it was a clever disguise for something else. Arthritis maybe?

"Had to have these ol' knees fixed when I got back from 'Nam."

Hmmm … a Viet Nam vet. Some place to start.

A ping pong table for two in "The Patio", a plastic curtain between us in a plastic cubicle. I couldn't wait to take my hot mask off. "Rufus" seemed to hesitate before removing his mask.

"Rufus, the first thing I have to ask you is – what is your real name? The sister over there told me that they started calling you 'Likka Sto' Rufus' to distinguish you from 'Drug Sto' Rufus.'"

It was a real surprise to see this man's face, to study the expressive lines. He looked Ethiopian to me, with the aquiline nose, the sexual mouth and firm chin line. He looked to be about sixty or maybe seventy, old enough to be my great grandfather.

"You ask a lot of questions, huh?"

"Maybe. I've found the best way to get answers is to ask questions."

"My government name is Melvin Montaigne Dixon the Third…"

"What do people mean when they say, 'My government name is?'"….

"Where are you from, man? Everybody knows that your government name is the name in the FBI files, the name on your check and stuff like that."

"Well, in answer to the first part of your question, I'm from Chicago …."

"Me too," he mumbled in his throat. It didn't seem that his voice suited his face, with all of the gravel.

"Really?"

"Yeah, you don't believe me?"

He was constantly defending himself, constantly challenging me. Or something.

"Yeah, I believe you. What part of Chi?"

"Born on the Near Westside, Washburne and Racine. You know where that is?"

"O yeah, I know Chicago pretty well."

"Born on the Near Westside, when it was ALL Negro-Black, lived there all my life 'til I joined the army."

The Vietnam war, of course. We sat there looking at each other for a few beats, two ex-Windy City guys.

The waitress interrupted our silence.

"Tea and coffee, anything else?"

"Uhh, Ruf… Melvin, you want anything else?"

"You can call me Rufus, that's what everybody else calls me. Yeahhh, I'd like something else. Let me see the menu."

Interesting dude, really interesting. I studied him as he studied the menu. He took his time before making a choice.

"I'll take this fish stew. It's got lots of fish in it, right?"

"Yessir, plenty of fish."

"Good. I'll take that. You're paying for this, right?"

"The whole thing." I ordered a couple adobo chicken rolls. We went back into the silent mode for a minute or two. Melvin, uhhh, Rufus wasn't the type to blabber.

He gave me the impression of being in a counter punch posture, all of the time.

"So, you like fish a lot, huh?"

"I do. And Tarzan likes fish too. Like most cats, I guess."

"Bet he's at home waiting for you to come home with the goodies."

"Nawww, ain't no telling where Tarzan is, he comes and goes."

"That's the way most tom cats are."

"How do you know he's a tom cat?"

"Well, just from what you just said, about Tarzan coming and going."

"Yeah, you got that right, he's a tom awright."

The adobo rolls were delicious, and I could tell that Rufus was enjoying his fish stew. Half thru our "lunch," I decided to dig a little deeper into this feisty little man's psyche.

"So, you got drafted for Viet Nam …?"

I felt like I had said something nasty to him, from the way the corners of his mouth curled down. He stopped eating and stared off into the distance. I felt like he had left the scene.

"Yeahhh, I got drafted, drafted to go over there and kill up a bunch of little brown men and women for the Big White Man."

I had struck a chord. This dude was bitter as Hell. What was it the great Muhammad Ali once said? "Ain't no Viet Cong ever called me a nigger, why should I go over there and fight them?"

Rufus was constantly keeping me off balance. I debated going into the Viet Nam war thing with him, but it seemed that he had said everything he wanted to say in one sentence. "Lunch" over. Now what?

"You going back to the liquor store?"

"Nawww, I've finished with that for today, I usually put in about three hours, from eleven 'til two. That's it."

He made it sound like a job, a J.O.B. Three hours a day, from eleven 'til two. Panhandler's hours.

"What made you decide to handle in front of the liquor store?"

He cocked his head to one side, as though he couldn't hear too well.

"Nobody ever asked me nothing like that. The simple answer is simple; drunks and semi-drunks are much more generous than sober people. I could stand in front of this restaurant and starve to death."

I couldn't really put my finger on it, how I felt about what he said about people going in and out of the liquor store. Was he calling me a drunk, a semi-drunk? I had to let it pass, the dude moved past me real fast, emotionally.

"So, you're going back home?"

"I'm going back to my space."

"I'll give you a lift."

I gave peripheral notice of the "likka sto' gang". They made an effort to pretend <u>not</u> to be curious, but I could tell from the joint going 'round seemed to be in suspended animation that they were <u>very</u> curious about what was happening.

15

Melvin Montaigne Dixon a.k.a. "Likka Sto' Rufus" was hanging out with this young brother from Nowhere. I could read the wheels clanking around in their skulls. Who is this brother? What's the deal?

None of this seemed to matter to Rufus. He did his hip dip-ripped-knees-giddy up hitch to my V.W.…. He stood at parade dress, looking at my ancient car for a few beats before he folded himself inside.

"You know something, Willie? …."

I was a bit tripped out to hear him call me by my "government name". I thought he had forgotten it.

"What's that, Rufus?"

"I think you must be – either an FBI agent, a Russian spy or one of these weirdass African-American writers."

"I'm one of these weirdass African-American writers."

"I knew it, I knew it! When you kept on asking me these weirdass questions – I knew you were a weirdass brother, but I didn't know you were a writer too."

The brother had worn me out. All I could think of was well chilled gin 'n ginger beer with a lot of ice. I had had enough for one afternoon.

"Rufus, I'm going to drop you off – where?"

He pointed straight ahead and then to the left thru an alley behind the shops that faced the mall.

"Right here. This is me."

I stared at the tent erected in the fenced in area behind Mr. Kim's liquor store. It was a fairly spacious tent, one of the kind that you could stand up in, a safari tent. It tripped me out.

"This is where you are?" Sounded like a silly ass question, but I asked it anyway.

"This is where I am," was the answer, without any other explanations or comments. And then, from the corner of my left eye, I caught the furtive approach of a large black tom cat. Tarzan.

"I'll never be able to figure out how he knows I'm bringing him some food home, but he knows it. And that's the only time he shows up."

"Why do you call him Tarzan?"

It didn't take a lot to imagine Rufus smiling behind his mask.

"'Cause he's a swinger. He's free. I can't pet him 'cause he ain't into that. And, he's Deep. Watch him take a couple nips of this fish stew. He might dig it or he might turn up his nuts and piss in it."

I drove away from Rufus' place thinking about a lot of stuff that would help me with "The Deadly Cult"

CHAPTER 3

"The Deadly Cult"

By Willie West

I went home, made my drink, studied my outline to figure out where I was in my manuscript.

"This latter-day plague was killing whole populations of people, whilst those weirdass Republicans had just spent four stuttering, mendacious nights trying to con the American public into giving this dumb ass fascist racist maniac narcissist another four years to destroy the "American Experiment.""

I sat at my desk, sipping and thinking. The thought literally lit me up – ask Rufus what he thinks. The second the fire flamed up in me I knew what I wanted to do, but immediately recognized how hard it was going to be to get this brother's cooperation. How would I go at him? What could I say to him? What if he didn't support my premise?

We hadn't talked a lot about politics during our "lunch" at the Filipino place. What if he didn't want to talk to me period? Time to talk to ZiZi.

❦

"Hey sweetheart, hope I'm not waking you up or anything...?"

"Willie, this is a really pleasant surprise, to be cliché about it. No, you're not waking me up or anything. As a matter of fact, I was just thinking about you."

"Good thoughts, I hope."

"Cut the bullshit, Willie. I know you. You wouldn't be calling me at ten thirty to solicit messages of affection. What's happenin'?"

We both started laughing at the same time. I loved that about ZiZi, bullshit had a narrow threshold.

"Awright awright, if you want to know the real reason why I called?"

"If you don't tell me right now, I'm going to hang up on you."

Lawd H' mercy/Eshu/Jesus! I had called exactly the right person. I sensed a bit of Rufus in ZiZi, as farfetched as that might sound. ZiZi was real.

"Well, as you know, I'm writing this novel ..."

"'The Deadly Cult', love that title."

"I'm pretty far into it, like a couple hundred pages, before I began to feel a little bit uneasy with the P.O.V. I was using. The more I thought about it the more I felt that I could say what I wanted to say thru another person."

"I got it, so?"

"So, I came up with this idea of interviewing, talking with an iconoclastic dude like 'Likka Sto' Rufus'."

"You mentioned him when you were up here. Sounds like he would be the ideal voice for you. What's the problem?"

"Actually, I can't say what the problem is, or what the problem is going to be because I haven't approached him yet."

"He's got you a little bit intimidated, huh?"

"Well, uhhh, I wouldn't put it quite like that. But what if he's a red hot MAGA Republican?"

Her sultry low-down laughter made me feel like trying to hug her body thru the 'phone.

"You won't know 'til you find out, will you?"

"I think I understand what you're saying."

"Just so you won't have to guess. Level with the dude, tell him what you're doing, where you're coming from. All he can do is say yea or nay. If he says 'nay,' you go to plan B."

"ZiZi, I knew you would be the one with the answer to my prayer."

"And I knew, when I heard your voice, that you would be the answer to my prayer too."

19

"You're coming down to Long Beach on Friday evening?"

"I'll be there at 7:30 p.m. I've been missing you like mad."

"I've been missing you more. See you Friday at 7:30."

I closed up my cell and stared at the calendar above my desk. Sunday. Damn, six whole days to wait for my love to come down.

"Conversations" with Rufus

I spent the rest of the evening, 'til about 1:00 a.m., going thru my outline making sure that I had a cohesive "map" to work with. I felt certain, if Rufus agreed to work with me, that I would have a serious program laid out.

It hurt a little to have to trash some of the stuff I had worked so hard on. But I felt I had to re-design some things to suit the "Likka Sto' Rufus" personality.

Would he ask me to pay him? Should I offer to pay him? And if I offered to pay him, how much should I offer?

I was spinning circles around in my head and I didn't even have a prospective publisher in mind. Offhand I couldn't even think of a publisher who would be interested in the kind of book I had in mind. I had to eliminate Hollow Day Publishers, the people who had published five of my novels because they were strictly about "Urban Fiction," or "Street Corner Lit".

In addition to everything else, I wasn't absolutely certain that I could write about what I had in the back of my mind. I had to cancel that thought out right away, or else I would wind up with a case of writer's block before I started writing.

Before flaming out, I decided to take ZiZi's advice – "Level with the dude, tell him what you're doing, where you're coming from. All he can do is say yea or nay. If he says "nay," you go to plan "B"."

I went to sleep, impatient for tomorrow to come.

Three hours a day. From eleven to two. "Panhandler's hours." I deliberately waited until 1:30, to make certain that I wouldn't interfere with his schedule, that I would arrive on the scene at just the right time. I must've been holding my breath because it seemed like I exhaled a sigh of relief when I saw him in his usual position, a few yards away from the entrance to Mr. Kim's liquor store.

I parked in the 3rd parking row and sat there, studying the scene. From members of the "likka sto' gang" lounging around somebody's beat up Chevy, still doing their fugal argument/discussion at the far edge of the parking lot.

"Yo, Rufus, what's up, brother?"

I liked the way he took his time to reply. He was not someone who could be rushed to reply or anything.

"Oh, hey Willie, on your way to get some fire water, huh?"

"No, not today. I got another errand to run."

A beer bellied dude stutter stepped out of the liquor store, hugging a six-pack and paused, to give Rufus a few coins. Rufus handed the coins back.

"No good, big timer. No good, ain't nothing I can do with metal money, it's got to be paper. I've told you that before."

21

The beer guy looked embarrassed and peeled a bill out of his pocket.

"Uhh, sorry, brother man."

I had to smile. This dude was something else. He turned his "I am Black History" mask back to face me.

"Now, what is it you were saying?"

"Rufus, you really take care bidness, you know that?"

"Hey, this ain't no plaything with me, you know what I'm saying?"

"Yeah, I hear you. That's the reason I came to talk with you."

Once again my mask hid the smile on my face. This brother had suspicion written in both eyeballs.

"What about?"

"Why don't we have a cup of tea while I explain?"

"What time you got?"

"Quarter to two."

"Awright, I got fifteen more minutes."

I stood way off to one side, taking in the total picture. Obviously, it didn't matter to him whether or not anybody dropped more bread in his basket or not. So far as I could analyze things, it was much important that he should be in his self-designated place than anything else. Finally, after exactly fifteen minutes he hip limped over to me.

"Awright, what about this tea?"

I made a snap decision as we made our way to the Filipino place. Level with him, don't try to be cute about anything. The waitress remembered us.

"Oh, I remember you from the last time."

"Are you sure? We had masks on the last time."

I could hear the waitress giggle behind her mask. He was definitely a funny sort of dude, if you dealt with him long enough to get behind that sarcastic/dry humor exterior.

Thank God we could de-mask, so that I could see the expression on his face as I talked to him about what I wanted to do with him.

"You mean, you mean you just want to talk with me and write about it? That's what you're saying to me?"

"That's what I'm saying to you."

He cradled his teacup in both hands and took a couple thoughtful sips.

"You know something, Willie, I think this is the first time in my life that I've ever had somebody ask me what I thought about any damned thing, interview me."

"No interview, Rufus, no interview. Just conversations. You may have as many questions for me as I have for you. We'll just have to see how this plays out."

"What if I say something you don't like? Will you leave that out?"

I knew I had to be patient with Rufus. He wasn't one of those people you could just rush into things.

"You can say anything you want to say, that's what I'm asking you to do."

He took a couple more sips of his tea. I could almost see the wheels spinning 'round in his head.

"What do you get out of this?"

"Good question. If it comes off as well as I think it will, I'll have a book, the kind of book I want. You know the old saying – 'If you can't find the book you want to read, go write one.'"

He thought that was funny enough to give up a sarcastic smile.

"And what about me, what do I get?"

"My girlfriend is an attorney, I'll have her draw up a contract that makes us partners, fifty per cent straight up the middle from whatever the book makes. I have to warn you, these kinds of books are a hard sell. But then you can never tell, you might wind up with a best seller."

He shook his head slowly, from side to side, as though he couldn't believe what he was hearing.

"You know, this is kinda funny, here I am a seventy-year old man about to become famous …."

"Whoaaa! Hold on Rufus, I didn't say that you were going to become famous or anything like that."

"I know I know, I was just yankin' your cord a little bit."

There, he was doing it again. I had to stay alert.

"Incidentally, what's up with Tarz'?"

"I always call him by his full name."

Ooppss. "So, what's up with Tarzan? How did he like his fish stew?"

"He liked it so much he licked the bowl clean."

"You think he might like some more?"

"Maybe he would, but I ain't gonna spoil his ass. He's back on the canned cat food, beginning right now."

I paid the check and we strolled; our heads filled with the journey to come.

"Give you a lift?"

"Nawww, I'm gonna run into the market and pick up this cat food. When do you want to get back together?"

"How about tomorrow, same time?"

"Yeah, that's cool. One last question, Willie?"

"Yeah, what?"

He had a really intense look in his eyes as he stared over the brim of his mask.

"Why me, Willie, why me?"

"Why not you, Rufus, why not you?"

And that's where we left it for the moment.

❦

"ZiZi, how you doing, sweetheart?"

"Much better, talking to you."

"I'm really looking forward to seeing you Friday."

"I'm looking forward to seeing you more."

"Well, we'll see about that."

"ZiZi, I just wanted to tell you that I had a meeting with Rufus. I took your advice and I leveled with him."

"That's great! I'm glad that he's cool with your idea."

"I think he has a few reservations, but basically I feel that he's all in. But I do need a little favor."

"Name it."

"I need a contract for what I want to do with him. It should be a fifty-fifty for any royalties we might make from the sale of the book. Radio, T.V., screenplay/movie … whatever."

"I know what you need, I'll bring it on Friday. Anything else?"

"Yes, but I can't discuss it on the phone."

"You're very naughty, you know that?"

"Yes, I do know."

"See ya on Friday."

"'Night baby."

I almost re-dialed her number because I had forgotten to say, "I love you, ZiZi." O well, next time. Meanwhile, let me get busy on this free form outline that I want to use with Rufus.

My idea was to simply talk with Rufus, not to "interview" him, but to draw him out, let him blow his soul. Somehow, he gave me the impression it was something that he could do without too much effort.

He was not one of those brothers who was stuck in a certain groove – "Know what *ahm* sayin'?" "Know what *ahm* sayin'?" "Know what *ahm* sayin'?" -- and he was certainly up to date on all of the present-day madness. Plus, the past-latter day madness. Wearing a face mask with "**I am Black History**" said a whole load of things.

I almost thought myself into a catatonic state, my ball point poised a half inch above the long yellow legal pad in on my desk. And then it fell in on me, just the way those things are apt to do when you simply unfreeze your creative self. I pictured Rufus as a four-season creature – a Spring-Summer-Autumn-Winter.

He was 70, that's what the man said. What that said to me, as a baby of twenty-eight, was that he was, like in the Early Autumn of his life. Once again, the catatonic state locked me away from myself for awhile.

The unfreezing happened gradually. I would have to pull some background out of Rufus, in order to establish some foundation for him being the way he is. But I was still determined not to get into that traditional – Where were you? When were you? Etc, etc, etc.

Some things were unavoidable. We had spent hundreds of years of our lives without masks on and then what happened? Must do some pre-mask. I was seeing us going thru lifetimes in a few months, from April 2020 to November 2020. I settled my head on that time frame.

What if Rufus didn't agree with my "outline"? I would have to risk that. I definitely felt a little crazy about assuming that Rufus was as anti-Trump as I was. I would have to risk that too.

What if the brother was in the Uncle Ben Carson-Cameron (the Kentucky Black son of McConnell), Clarence Thomas (Uncle Thomas), Negrocentric sons/daughters of the Confederate lovers of Black Enslavement. Or whatever any reasonable person could call them.

I decided to say fuck it. And go on and write the prologue of what I was going to write about, no matter what. And flesh out the outline as we went along. A weird gamble? Well, the brother had called me weird.

CHAPTER 4

Miles Davis's "Sketches of Spain" kept running thru my brain as I had my first talk with Rufus, the following day I had to wait for Rufus to "finalize" his time in front of the liquor store. Truth be told, I was beginning to have weird feelings about how this was going to work out. What if I had chosen the wrong subject/character for my idea?

I think Rufus put me at ease when I parked in the restaurant lot (near my car) and we went in for our tea. They were ready for us – "Your table is there."

Rufus strolled in as though this was where he was meant to be.

"You payin' for this, right?"

I assured him that I was going to take the check before he began to unravel...

"The brother drank all of the Kool-Aid. I'm talking about this brother down there in Kentucky. How could he push the stuff forward that he was pushing, when he knew different? When he knew that he was pushing the wrong version of the truth. Poor Breanna Taylor."

"You're talking about Daniel Cameron, the Attorney General of Kentucky?"

"Call him any name you want to call him...."

(Let me go back up the page for a bit. Back to when I said that I was recording my first talk with Rufus. I was not doing scribble-scribble-steno stuff with the brother. I had to make him understand that he could talk to me, he could talk at me. He could just talk in general, and I would transcribe it, in other words, put it in publishable words.)

"You mean, in ways that the White folks can understand it?"

"Yeah, I guess that's what I'm saying."

"Then why didn't you say that?"

27

The brother was in his usually combative state. Good. Our waitress escorted us to our table. – The Salamat Po restaurant.

"Tea?" She asked.

"Yes m'am, I'd like a cold glass of iced tea. I don't know what this guy wants."

The waitress was a giggler, I could hear the sound behind her mask. And I could tell that she was smiling from the twinkle in her eyes. Rufus had that effect on people whenever he turned his charm on.

It was always a pleasure to "de-mask."

"Rufus, you were saying something about this guy, Cameron, the Black Attorney General in Kentucky?"

"I was talking about all of 'em, Willie, all of 'em. All of the Black Trumpido Republicans. I remember Cameron because he got up and spoke at that virtual whatchucallit. I can't exactly recall what he said, but I can tell you this – it was obvious that he had swallowed a whole lot of the Kool-Aid."

I have to say, I took a deep breath and exhaled a sigh of relief. It was going to be alright; Rufus was not a Trump guy. Thank God. We sipped our tea for a few moments. I knew my guy well enough now, to know that I couldn't have a pre-arranged agenda, I had to go with the flow.

"What's with those Black dudes anyway? How can they go for the Accordion Man's game?"

"The Accordion Man, who's that?"

"Trump. Ever notice how he looks like he's about to start playing an accordion, with his hands doing that squeeze box routine, 'specially when he starts lying, which is all the time."

We shared smiles. "Accordion Man", I could see a whole chapter on the Trump body language.

"I notice you don't have a notebook or anything. How are you going to remember what we talk about?"

"I won't remember each and every word, but I'll have the idea, the core of it, and that's what I'll write after every session we have. Oh, incidentally, my lady is coming down here from San Francisco this weekend and she'll have a contract …."

He stroked his low bristled goatee and cocked his head to one side, studying me.

"Willie, I'm beginning to think that you are somewhat serious about this."

"I am, Rufus, I am."

SPRING

"Willie, first thing I think we have to look at, is where I came from. I know we're both from Chicago, but there's a whole bunch of different Chicagos. I'm coming from a 70-year old Westside and you're coming from a 28-year Southside Chicago, both Black/African-American, but in a lot of ways, like different tribes.

I lived in Jew Town, that's what the people, the Jews, named the section I lived in. The Jewish guys, were merchants, bidness men. They weren't into White Supremacy and all of that craziness. They were into selling. Growing up I didn't think a lot about who these people were, where they came from. They were there and they sold us the stuff we wanted and they were polite, called us 'Mr.' and 'Mrs.', said 'Thank you', gave us credit 'til the next paycheck.

You have to remember, we were coming out of low-grade Southern slavery. Nobody had ever been nice to us. When I look back on it, I think some of us treated each other worse than the Jews, the only White folks we knew.

I'm not going to make excuses for anybody or try to soft soap anything. But I can tell you this, after having read a couple books on group psychology and other stuff, I can definitely point a straight finger at the source of a lot of the negative stuff that went on."

[He was on a roll. I felt like a blessed man, an African-American writer who was being given the street learned knowledge of another era, and God only knows whatever else. I was not about to stop the flow.]

"People carried switchblade knives. Everybody had a knife. Some people had guns. Lots of chips on lots of shoulders. My theory is that a lot of this anger, this nega-tivity came from the fact that most of us was from Down South.

What that means is that so many folks had been treated so bad by them racist snake dogs down there, it was like they were mad at the world for what had happened to them. Don't dispute what I'm saying; I know what I'm talking about."

"Rufus, I'm not disputing anything, I'm just listening." The brother could be somewhat exasperating.

"My mother was from Little Rock, Arkansaw and my Daddy was from Yazoo City, Miss'ssippi. And I can tell you, as a matter of fact, that they had a lot of that nega-tivity in them. If they weren't playing the blues and fighting with each other, they were fighting with other people.

I think it was pretty much like that up and down the street we lived on. Life was hard. But right there, in the middle of this ghetto jungle, people could be sweet as pie. It was like the whole neighborhood was bipolar or something.

As you can see, I was small, so I had to be twice as mean and vicious as the bigger kids. It meant I had to hold my mug. You know what that means?"

"I hope so."

He paused in his narrative to tilt his head in that curious way he had.

"Willie, you know something?"

"No, what?"

"You got an odd sense of humor." That was all he said before he continued his narrative.

"Yeah, I can't think of a week, from the time I was seven – eight, up until I was about fifteen or so, when I wasn't fighting somebody about something."

"Survival of the fittest."

"You got that right. I was the fittest. And when I was fifteen I bought this switchblade. I was tired of punching and wrestling; it was time to start cutting. That's also when I started getting in a little trouble, now and then. You think we could get them to serve us some of those ado-bos, you know? With the chicken inside. I checked yours out the other day and it looked pretty good."

I signaled to the waitress.

"Miss, we'd like a couple chicken adobo rolls and more tea, please?"

"And please tell us what your pretty name is, so we won't have to call you — waitress."

"My name is Lola."

"My goodness, that is such a pretty name."

I think I could see the poor girl blush behind her mask. He definitely could turn the charm spigot on whenever he wanted to.

"How's Tarzan?"

"I don't want to talk about that rascal, going around shitting behind my tent. Where was I?"

"You were talking about growing up with a knife in your hand on the Westside, getting into 'a little trouble, now and then.'"

"You got a good memory, Willie, a good memory. Yeahh, I did a little time in three juvenile homes before I was 19. Nineteen years old, going on 39, getting ready to go do some big time in the Big House. That's what they used to call the penitentiary.

Brothers used to call to each other across the street and ask; "You been in the Big House yet?" It was like a Rite of Passage thing for us. No big thang. I think it was my Daddy who saved me from Big Time in the Big House.

On one of our visits to see him in the pen, Statesville Penitentiary, Joliet, Illinois. Ever been there?"

"I've been there a few times; I had an uncle and three cousins who did some time...."

"So, you know what I'm talking about."

Lola made a deft move and placed four adobo rolls in a serving platter on our table, a couple smaller plates in front of us, poured hot tea in my cup and gave Rufus a fresh glass of ice tea. We both stared at her dance-like movements.

"Anything else? She asked.

"Not at the moment, Miss Lola, thank you."

We looked at each other with a male chauvinist understanding of the scene. This is a real cutie pie.

"On this particular visit, Daddy finishing up a ten-year bit for sale and possession of cocaine, robbing the Third National Bank, burglarizing the White House; I can't remember all the crimes he had committed."

31

I had to laugh: "...robbing the Third National Bank, burglarizing the White House." This brother had lots of imagination.

"Melvin, you see where I am?" That was the way he started in on me.

"Yeah, Dad, I see where you are."

"And this is where you gonna be too, in the next couple years or so, if all the info I'm receiving about you is correct. I'm not going to ask you if my info is correct or not because you'll just lie. So, I'm not going to get into that.

Just let me say this, you can lump it and dump it, as the saying goes. Or you can use it to make a better life for yourself."

"You got to understand; My Daddy was a coldblooded dude. He took as good as he got and I never once heard him whine like a lil' bitch. So, when he got serious on me, it meant something."

"Melvin," he said, "I am 42 years old and I have spent exactly half of my life in these White folks' prisons. I say White folks' prisons 'cause Black folks have never owned any prisons in America. You know what I'm sayin'?"

"All I could do was nod. I had never thought about who owned the prisons."

"21 years of my life, son." That flipped my head. "Son?" He usually just called me Melvin.

"21 years of my life living in a cage like an animal. Think about that. In a cage, like being in a zoo. The owners of the cages can come and feed you whenever they want, to feed you whatever they want to, treat you any kind of way they want to.

And you can't do shit about it because you are a prisoner, you are a captive and the owner of the prison, the White man, has complete control of your ass. He can even regulate the time you can jack off. Or fuck your fellow prisoner in the ass."

"Willie, you talk about some scary shit. I sat on the other side of this barrier (they didn't have all of the sophisticated electronic stuff back then), staring at his mouth, my jaw dropped down to here. I was trying as hard as I could to look brave, not to cry, but he broke me down."

"You a bad little dude, I know that, but that won't save your ass in here. What you have to understand is real simple – you're small and some of them are huge. We have a brother in here that looks like 'King Kong', as a matter of fact they call him 'King Kong', behind his back, and he specializes in busting open little asses, asses like your ass, Melvin."

"I remember, during this visit, we stopped talking, he stopped talking for a long minute, just looking at each other. He had convinced me, with one graphic fairy tale, that I did not want to be in 'King Kong's' harem."

"Well, what should I do, Dad?"

"Join the Army."

"That's what he said – 'Join the Army.'"

I checked off the place earlier when he had told me he was drafted.

SUMMER

"Maybe I was a few months short of the legal date of enlistment, but everybody seemed to ignore all of the technical stuff. I was twenty years old and they needed some cannon fodder, body fuel. That's what I picked up on right away.

On the other hand, as frantic as they were to have bodies to burn; they also had these weird things going on, like being willing to encourage the best to try to move ahead. I had not ever experienced that kind of stuff before. Remember, this is how Colin Powell became what he became.

The freaky dookey thing about all of this was one big Question. If the Army could 'graduate' individuals on the basis of how much they deserved to be where they were, then why couldn't we do the same in civilian society? That really puzzled me.

What's it called? I know you know the word."

"I would call it a meritocracy."

"Yeahhh, that's it. Meaning that you can rise or fall on your own merits."

"That's exactly what it means."

"You don't have to reaffirm what I just said; I know what I'm talking about."

I had to smile. The brother was so, so contentious, so quick to take offense. I thought – he might be bi-polar.

"Now don't get me wrong. I did not fall in love with the Army. The first thing that bugged the shit out of me was that they got up too early.

I could never figure out why we had to get up at 6 a.m. to go marching somewhere. We could've got up at 8 a.m. and done the same damned thing. Like I said, I could really see that there was a chance for a Black man to make it, to be respected, to be somebody in the military.

Even though the White folks wouldn't think he was shit out of the military. So many contradictions happening at the same time. It was cool for us to be marching 'round in our fatigues, dodging rattlesnake bites and learning how to shoot people dead, but the usual suspects didn't want to see us downtown in our Class A uniform, or to see us, period."

"Where were you stationed?"

"Fort Gordon, Georgia. And that's another bone that stuck in my throat. Think you might like to order some more tea and another one of these ado-bo rolls, they mighty tasty."

I signaled to Lola – another round of the same. She was definitely on the job.

"You say Fort Gordon was a bone in your throat?"

"Yeah, why wouldn't it be? Why in the hell would they have a U.S. Army post named after a Confederate general? I thought they lost 'Duh Wahr'. That's what he called it – 'Duh Wahr'". He paused to give Lola a warm smile as she placed more rolls and tea on our table.

"Rufus, I notice you don't eat much."

"One meal a day is enough for somebody my age. Look at me and look at my fatso friends hanging 'round out there."

There was definitely a contrast. Rufus was small, lean, looked like he could've been an Ethiopian long-distance runner for sure. The "likka sto' Gang", a hundred yards to our left, clustered as usual, having their usual fugal half argument/conversations, were definitely on the obese side.

"You know, that's one of the things I really don't like about America…."

"What's that?"

"The contradictory stuff. It really socked me in the head at Fort Gordon. I just couldn't get used to the racism. On the post everybody had <u>almost</u> a fair shot to make rank, be somebody. But the minute you stepped outside the concern; you were just considered to be just another nigger.

I had taken my Daddy's suggestion and joined the Army. Obviously, he was trying to save my life from my doing the same thing he had done. I understood all that, I really did. But that racism stuff really got on my left nerve.

"'We're asking our Negro soldiers not to wear their uniforms into Augusta, it upsets some people.'"

Here I am, a soldier in the American Army, and this crackerass sergeant is telling/asking me and the other brothers in our company not to go into town wearing our uniforms … because it might piss off the local crackers.

I thought I was going to puke on my spit shined boots when I heard him say this insane shit."

I stared at this little hard bitten warrior with re-newed respect. I had definitely picked the right moral agent for the story I wanted to tell. He looked like he wanted to cry. I slid in as gently as I could.

"Rufus, let me get this straight. You're not going to tell me that you didn't know racism existed before you enlisted."

"O hell yeah, I knew it existed. Hell yeah, but I was only acquainted, had been only acquainted with low down, street level racism. That's when the police drive by a corner and shout out, 'Awright you niggers! Gimme that corner!'"

"That was expected. I didn't expect to go into the U.S. Army and they tell me I should be prepared to give up my life for my country. And the White folks were telling me, at the same time, your life doesn't mean shit. I was into the Black Lives Matter concept way back when.

As a matter of fact, I was on the verge of deserting, that's right! You heard me! I was on the verge of deserting!"

People at nearby tables (socially distancing) turned curious glances our way. I hand gestured for Rufus to lower his rant. He gave me a mean look, but he did lower his voice.

"I was on the verge of deserting. I had suffered thru enough of this crap. It was 1965 and I had put in a full year, I had three more to go. I was planning to hat up."

"Where were you going to desert to, where were you going to go?"

"For a hot minute, I thought about Bulgaria…"

"Why Bulgaria?"

"I just figured that that would be one of the least likely places they would come looking for my little black ass."

We traded conspiratorial smiles. Yeah, maybe you got something there.

"But, wouldn't you know it? Exactly three days before I was to about to make my move, they woke us up in the middle of the night for an ID/dog tag – short arm check."

"Short arm? To see if your arms were too short?"

He had a completely soundless way of laughing. He laughed so hard he squeezed tears out of his tightly closed eyes. So, what the hell is so funny?

"Willie, Willie, Willie, a short arm inspection is when they have you line up, pull your dick out of your shorts for the doctor, or the medic, so that they can see if you have a venereal disease."

"Oh." What else could I say?

"What you have to remember is that a whole bunch of these young crackers hadn't even started taking a shower regularly, 'til they got in the Army. And a whole bunch of them had untreated VDS, hangovers from having sex with their sisters, their cousins, whoever."

I didn't make a skeptical face, after all he had been there and back. I was beginning to clearly understand that I had to keep him on track.

"What was reason for the ID/dog tag, uhhh, short arm inspection?"

"We were being sent to some place called Viet-Nam."

❧

CHAPTER 5

"It took us like forever to get to some place called Guam, 'way out in the middle of the ocean, somewhere between East Hell and No Where. What do you call it, surreal?"

"Yeah, surreal."

"That's what I said. The whole trip was surreal. It was like we had been transported to a jungle on the moon. We landed in the middle of the afternoon and the first impression I had of the place, of this Viet-Nam, was that it was one of the funkiest places I had ever been in my whole entire life.

Funky-stanky and hot as hell. I forgot the name of the airport, but I'll always remember the sight of this group of soldiers who were walking to get into a 'plane waiting to take them away. It was almost like a game of 'come 'n go'. We were coming and they were going.

Let me tell you something, Willie, these dudes looked like they had just been pulled thru a pile of roach snot."

It was one of those times when I wished that I brought my notebook with me. "Roach snot." I wasn't likely to forget that.

"It took me approximately four days to really understand why. The people going looked the way they did. We were checked in, given a barrack to sleep in. Some little crooked mouthed 2d Lt. gave us something called an 'orientation' the next day.

"We're here to help the Vietnamese people secure their freedom. That's one of the many dumbass things he said. He's saying this to us; nine Black men in this company. There was also a few Latino guys, two Asians and the rest was po' White kids from places like Cottonville, Miss'ssippi, Athens, Georgia, Tough, Alabama ("hits named Tough 'cause that's what it is").

None of us were exactly free. And we were there to 'help the Viet Nam people secure their freedom.' The hy-pocrisy was sky high, from Day One.

Day Two. We were slogging thru these fields that were fertilized by human shit. I was, how would you say it? Appalled."

It took me a second or two to realize that the brother was being sarcastic. You could never tell about Rufus.

"I hated Viet Nam and the Viet Namese for all of the three years I was trapped there. And that's the description I can use to describe what happened to me. I got trapped. Let me give you an example of what I mean ..."

[I think this is as good a place as any to weave in a few dynamics. The people in the restaurant knew Rufus. They had seen him in his position as the panhandler in front of the liquor store, just a few stores away.

He was not well dressed, and he was a bit of a loud talker. Plus, I found out, after a couple meetings at the Salamat Po, that he was a long-winded talker once you got him started. After our fourth meeting I made a surreptitious apology to Lola, the waitress, for occupying a table so long.

"No problem," she whispered back, "he's a veteran, no problem."

I thought that was really nice, really nice to be like that. I always tipped well to show my gratitude.]

"You say you were trapped?"

"That's what I said, trapped. First off, it took me awhile to really realize where I was. I studied this big map they had in the office. I was somewhere deep in the middle of Laos, Cambodia and God only knows where. The closest place I could recognize as being somewhere near civilization was Hawaii.

Like I said, I hated Vietnam and Vietnamese and I felt I had a right to. That was before a couple of these Conscious brothers in my unit started talking to me radi-calizing me."

"Look, brother Melvin, don't you see what's happenin'. We over here fightin' the White devils battle for them. They want to have control of the heroin that's comin' out of this Triangle – Vietnam, Cambodia and Laos. This is the American White Devil's Opium war, just like the English Opium war."

"To be truthful, I didn't exactly understand what they were talking about, concerning the English Opium war and all of that. But I soon got to understand something about the drug scene, on a personal level.

I had been in the country exactly six days before I smoked my first joint. I had smoked 1, I mean, who ain't smoked weed? But this was different herb, real different. I had a joint on a Saturday and I didn't come back to myself 'til the following Tuesday. 'Super Weed' we called it. It didn't take me long to start having problems. Number one, the 1st Sergeant hated me. He was one of those unreconstructed crackers from 'way down south, Miss'ssippi, I think.

And he was all over my lil' black ass from Day one."

"Private, I don't know why they allowed you to volunteer to be in my Army!"

"Maybe it's 'cause it ain't your Army, it's the United States Army."

"Watch yo' mouf soldier! Do you know who you're talkin' to?!"

"Yeah, I know."

He seemed to think that I was some kind of thug or something just because I was from Chicago.

"We won't be havin' any shenanigeens from none of the gangstas from Chicago!"

That was one of his standard raps. The 98th Civil Affairs Company had nine brothers in the whole unit. Two hundred and twelve people, nine of us. We were overseas in Viet Nam, in a war zone, but a whole lot of that ugly racism had been imported, along with everything else.

Lots of people can't imagine what it was like to be over there, supposedly to fight for somebody else's freedom, whilst we were still having problems trying to be free at home.

Pardon my French, but it was a bitch of a situation."

"How was it a bitch of a situation, Rufus, tell me?"

He stared at some point in the distance for a moment before he spoke.

"I'll tell you. First of all, nobody that I knew believed that we were supposed to be there. We didn't believe it. The Vietnamese didn't believe it. Nobody like the brother said, it was the White Devil's war to control the flow of the dope coming out of Laos, Cambodia and Viet Nam. That's the only reason I could see. That's the only thing. Every time we went out on patrol, and somebody got hit or killed, I would think – for what?

It got to be crazier and crazier every day. We would go out into the jungle, Black and White, and fight side by side. But when we got back from the jungle and went into Saigon on a weekend pass, the Whites went to the "White" sector and we went to "Harlem".

Yeah, that's right, segregation, my friend, segregation. I have to be honest and tell you, straight up none of us, the brothers, wanted to be hanging out with a bunch of rowdy, red necked, crazy ass White men anyway. They couldn't even dance.

Yeah, while our folks at home were catching hell trying to vote, we were over in Viet Nam to fight for some people's right to be free, to vote.

I can't really put my finger on it, but toward the end of my second year in 'Nam, that's what we called it, by the end of my second year I snapped.

I had seen people step on mines right in front of me and have their balls blown off. The Viet Cong, the people we were fighting but hardly ever saw, had come up with a cute little land mine that we called a 'jumping jack' because when it was triggered, it would toss up an explosive to about waist level and explode. Lots of people got de-balled from these 'jumping jacks'.

'Jumping jacks', punji sticks, sharpened bamboo slivers with buffalo dung on them, shit that caused instant infections. This is the kind of stuff happening in the field. It was just as bad in the city, in Saigon. You could be having a beer in the local bar and somebody might whip past on a motor scooter and roll a couple grenades inside."

"Sounds pretty horrible to me."

"That's what I'm trying to make you understand!"

I had learned how to go with the flow. I was beginning to have a very strong suspicion that Rufus was bi-polar. Or worse.

"All the stuff I'm telling you was bad, but I think the worse, the very worse-worse was …."

There was that pause again. I took a sip of my tea and waited.

"Let me put it this way, you wanna have a little nookie from time to time, 'specially if you've been in the field for a couple weeks and you haven't raped anybody. So, what do you do? You get your two-day pass to go into town, have a few beers and go to Mama San's pleasure palace to try to scrape a little bit of this cheese off your chest. That was the usual program for most dudes.

Maybe it was the Chicago in me, but I just couldn't see myself paying somebody to sell me some love. You know what I'm saying?"

I was forced to smile. The way this guy could mix things was truly fascinating. What did being from Chicago have to do with being a nookie buyer or not? O well…

"I almost dropped down on my knees when the news started leaking out. It seems that the Viet Cong had co-opted a few of the Mama Sans and put their own girls in the houses. As I understand it, some of these girls had been deliberately infected with some untreatable kind of V.D.

These Viet Cong prostitutes would infect the troops that came thru. As you can well imagine, that was very bad morale for the troops. A friend of mine, a medic, told me about dudes who were coming to him, their dickheads rotting off, for shots of Penicillin. Penicillin wouldn't do it. The V.D. was incurable. Like I said, I stayed away from buying some love. I drank some beer, smoked some weed and read a lot of books.

The kicker came later, when the story came out about these Viet Cong girls who had <u>volunteered</u> to be infected, so that they could infect American soldiers. I knew we were doomed to get our asses kicked out of 'Nam. I knew that after being there for a couple months. And then, when I found out about the poisoned nookie thing, I was 100% certain that we were doomed to defeat.

Anytime you have some people who would be willing to do something that cold, you may as well forget about trying to conquer them."

ZiZi looked like a dream come true. It seemed like the week I had been waiting for her had turned into a month. Well, maybe I'm exaggerating a little, but that's the way I felt.

She made me feel as though I had never been in love before. In many ways that was the honest to God truth. As a 28-year old

41

African-American man born in Chicago, I could own up to having been in bed with a few women, but this was the first time I felt love.

She melted into my arms as L.A.X. swirled around us.

"I have three days to be with you and I have that contract you wanted." That was what she said and it was the catalyst for one of the most gorgeous times I've ever had in my life.

There we were, in the middle of a plague, a few weeks away from deciding whether we were going to have a democracy (such as it was) or a dictatorship. Whether we were going to live or die, literally.

"I have three days to be with you." That's what she said. And that was all that mattered. We updated each other on our plague status as we gently undressed each other in my bedroom.

"I'm tested every other day because of my relationship to Vice-President Harris."

"She hasn't been elected yet…"

"She will be."

She was so upbeat, so hip about things.

"I can't imagine that you'd have me come down here and be germy…."

"You're correct, I'm negative. Since last week."

Truth be told, we sprawled out on my king-sized bed, making joke filled scenarios about us, our time, the Plague, and its effect on our lives.

"Sir, would you be kind enough to show me your negative pass, please?"

"Yes m'am, I will be kind enough to show you my negative ass…."

"Sir, I said – pass, not ass."

"Well then, m'am, I don't have any negative ass, I'm all positive."

We did a lot of that. I had moments, bright moments, when I felt that I was hallucinating. It had nothing to do with the fact that we had slowly undressed each other, the minute we closed my apartment door. I'm emphasizing "slowly" because we weren't into "quick get it done," we were into each other.

Friday evening, the time ZiZi had arrived, gradually gave birth to Saturday morning. I was still running my mouth when ZiZi said; "Uhhh, Willie, don't you think we ought to take a little nap?"

"Yeahh, why not?" I wasn't really sleepy, but I had to remember that my lover, my guest, had left a busy-busy San Francisco Friday to fly down into my ferociously loving arms.

I laid there, besides her, studying her profile, from head to toe, enjoying myself. I love this woman. That's what I whispered to myself before I wandered off into a ZiZi-filled dream.

We had decided to "camp" indoors, take a walk on the beach — "You know, I'm running back and forth across the bridge all the time, but I seldom have the opportunity to get close to the water."

"No problem here, lady, I can give you all of Long Beach."

"You're so kind."

We found an excuse to kiss every time we were within arm's distance from each other, which was often in my one bedroom apartment. We were a perfect fit. How many women did I know, have known, who would sit beside me on my sofa, sipping Oolong tea and listening to Gamelan music from Bali, the sarod and sitar from India, Orisha songs from Brooklyn, Cuba and Atlanta, Charlie Parker, Garth Brooks....

"You really like a spectrum of music, don't you?"

"Always have, it's all good."

We stayed away from the T.V. by unspoken — mutual agreement. Saturday afternoon. I had read the contract/agreement and found everything cool.

"I think this will be cool with him, but you can never tell, he has his ups and downs."

"Sounds like he's worth the effort you're putting into this ...."

"I think so." I showed her the rough outline, the pertinent notes I was taking after each one of our meetings.

"You'll have a chance to meet him this afternoon."

"I'm looking forward to it."

"Meanwhile...."

"You want a kiss?"

"Yes please."

"Hmmm, I like that — yes, please."

43

CHAPTER 6

I had planned it. Saturday afternoon, when Rufus got off (at 2 p.m. I remembered), I was going to give ZiZi and Rufus a Salamat Po dinner-treat. It was the only restaurant in the city that I felt at ease inside. Or outside. The cellophane/plastic cubicles did wonders for my confidence.

I drove past the liquor store twice. No Rufus.

"Maybe he decided not to do his thing today."

I halfway agreed with ZiZi, but I decided to check a little deeper.

"Hey, any y'all seen Rufus?"

"Naw, we ain't seen 'him."

Well, that was that. We didn't have Rufus with us, but we had an absolutely delightful dinner.

"You know, living in San Francisco, I get a chance to go to lots of Chinese restaurants. It seems that somebody is always having some sort of dinner at a Chinese restaurant. I've gone to enough of them to find out that the big lanterns in the ceiling, the fancy drapes and all of the rest does not automatically mean that they have great Chinese food. Sometimes they don't. I have to admit I've only had Filipino food a couple times…."

I relayed this info to Lola, who happened to be on duty.

"So, if I was trying to impress her with a good Filipino dinner – what should I order?"

"Don't worry about it; I will take care of it."

Now that's the mark of a great waitress. And she was true to her word. She started us off with this sort of sourish soup. And then led us all the way into a couple of perfectly grilled pompanos. Steamed rice and veggies on the side.

"Oohh fish! Willie, you know I love fish grilled like this."

A really gorgeous two hours. It didn't take long after we finished dinner that I began to have this thought ping thru my subconscious. This is the woman I want to marry, the woman I want to spend the rest of my life with. I can't begin to think that there is a more beautiful feeling in the world than the feeling of being in love, of being with someone you love.

We left the restaurant (I left a nice tip) and drove to the ocean. I had forgotten what the beach front was like on a Saturday afternoon, 'specially during the Plague. There were people everywhere, but in a strongly "nuclear" way. ZiZi noticed it.

"Looks like everybody is taking this thing seriously."

The 'nuclear" thing I'm talking about had to do with the ways people had spaced themselves from each other. And there were very few un-masked people running around. Miraculously, we found a parking space in Bixby Park, the park overlooking the beach.

We strolled the path down to the beach. The Pacific Ocean looked like a glassy pond with dimples.

"Willie, this is beautiful."

People passed us going uphill and I could imagine the smiles behind their masks because they spoke – "Hello!" and they had such friendly eyes.

We strolled the beach 'til we found a nice mound of sand to sit on. We sat and stared at the ocean for a long time. I loved that about ZiZi. That we could go to the ocean, sit there, stare at the water and not say a word, for long periods of time.

She was with me for the time she was with me and that was all that mattered. She was an "enabler".

She enabled me to think past, overdue bills, to focus on productive concerns, no Trump. I'll always remember the way she leaned back on her elbows when she said – "I don't think America is ready for a dictator. Of course, there are some White people in America who would welcome a White dictator, because they are deathly afraid of having people of color treat them the way they treated us.

Just goes to show you how little they know about us after all of these years. We're not like them.

We would never enslave White men, rape White women, or push breast feeding White babies into cages. We're too human for madness like that."

"So, let me ask you this…"

She gave her all in, intense look.

"What happens if Trump is re-elected?"

"Oh," she answered without hesitation, "I would kill myself, commit suicide."

I must've looked like someone who had been blasted between the eyes with an emotional brick. She squirmed over into my arms.

"Willie, Willie, I'm just joking sweetheart, I'm just joking. Don't worry he won't win."

The way she said it eased my distress. Have to admit, I went out there for a second or two.

Back to the pad. I made it a point of driving past the liquor store to see if Rufus was on duty. He wasn't. I was becoming a little concerned about the brother.

"Maybe he's hanging out with his lady." ZiZi's spin on his absence. O well, who knows?

We spent Sunday in bed, all day yes, angels did dance on the ceiling a few times, no doubt about that. But there was definitely more to it than that. We talked about dozens of things. We questioned each other about different things. We exchanged points of view.

One of them concerned the reality of African-American men voting for Trump.

"I've done more for the African-American community than any President since Abraham Lincoln." That's what the Trumpster said.

I had to admit, the thought of African-Americans voting for a racist, a White supremacist supporter, a devil who had tried to have five young Black and Brown men lynched/The Central Park Five, made me feel like puking. In addition to the disproportionate number of victims of the Plague who were African-Americans, who suffered because of his inept handling of the situation. Plus, his outright stoking of racial divisions.

"Willie, sweetheart, I totally agree with you, but we have to go way beneath the surface on this…"

This was a trait that I found in ZiZi that was absolutely great. She always seemed to be willing to take matters to a deeper level.

"I'd just like to give you three points, three conclusions why I feel a lot of young African-American males may be fuel for Trump's fire. Number one, sad to say, a lot of them are challenged by history. They don't know a lot about their history or anything else.

They don't read. They tend to be one dimensional in their perception of political stuff. If Kanye or Jay-Z or whoever says it's cool, then they go there and will not be persuaded otherwise.

Number two, despite the alternative reality that a Trump proposes – how many young Black men, and some not so young, have to be assassinated before the brother clearly understand/write 'Law and Order', meaning that police should be excused for shooting unarmed Black men and women.

Number three, I believe that some men, Black and otherwise simply dig Trump's pseudo machismo stance. They want to be defiant of the norms. The goofy thing about all of this is that they don't seem to understand how much they hurt themselves by giving aid and comfort to someone who clearly does not have their best interests at heart."

"So, what do you say to them? How can you help them see the light?"

"You can't say anything to them. They're stone deaf at this point, even after Trump has called their mothers 'bitches' and 'dogs.' And you can't help them see the light because they're totally blind now.

Willie, remember – there were 'Jews for Hitler'. Human beings are weird."

❦

By the time Monday morning rolled around (she was taking off for 'Frisco in the evening) we had made a number of Decisions.

"It'll take me about two months to clear my stuff up in 'Frisco. And I've three enthusiastic responses to my resume down here, looks like I'll be going with the Cochrand Brothers ...."

"I'm glad you decided to come down here because I was on the verge of coming up there to be with you."

"Willie West, you lyin' yo' ass off! Nothing on this planet would make you move to San Francisco, because you're deathly afraid of all those hills."

We laughed ourselves silly on that one. She knew her man. We laughed about that, but we got serious about the serious stuff.

"My parents left me a two story building and a couple lots in Beaumont, Texas. The properties are managed by the Wrangling Real Estate Management Corp. They send me a check for five grand every month."

"And there I was, thinking you were a starvin' artist. Sounds like the real estate people are cheating you. I have a couple real estate connections; I'll have them check into your stuff for you."

"Now then, how about you? Am I going to have to loan you a few grand to make you move?"

I loved the snarky way she looked at me after I asked my impertinent question.

"I don't think so. I usually clear between eighty or ninety thou a year and now, since I can't run away to Africa, Asia or Europe on vacations because of the plague, I'll probably be able to save a few bucks."

ZiZi sounded so logical, so reasonable.

"ZiZi, how about kids? You want twins the first year?"

"No lover, I would like for us to buy a nice house first. And then, we can start planning a family and it won't be twins, I can practically guarantee you that."

In between the light talk and the heavy talk, we were in each other's arms. She didn't want to go, and I didn't want her to go.

"ZiZi, why can't you reschedule until tomorrow night?"

"Willie, please baby, don't tempt me. I'm a working girl, I have to be at work at 9 a.m. tomorrow morning."

❦

Much as I hate to admit it, I felt a bit depressed for a couple days after my ZiZi left. We were going to be reduced to phone calls again for a few weeks. How long did she say it would take? A couple months? A couple lifetimes. O well …

Meanwhile, there was Rufus. I almost had an accident zipping into the mall when I spotted him standing in front of the liquor store. The liquor store regulars were in their usual positions, doing their circular firing-squad-argument-number.

I almost twisted my ankle getting out of the car to run over to him. "Yo Rufus, where you been, man?"

He had the same snarky expression on his face that ZiZi used. I was tempted to laugh.

"What am I s'posed to be doin' checkin' in or something?"

Same ol' Rufus. I sucked up to him with a shit eatin' grin.

"Nawww, nothing like that, my brother. My lady was down from San Francisco for the weekend, and we tried to hook up with you, but I guess we missed you."

While we're having this "explanatory conversation," a couple young sisters walked past on the way into the liquor store, their clothes and pores reeking of a skunky brand of marijuana.

"Uhhh, 'scuse me, Willie; so, what're y'all gonna do, just walk past me like you don't even see me standing here?"

I edged away from the scene by a few yards, to get a better angle on the situation. The two young women (neither one could've been older than twenty) approached Rufus respectfully, digging down into their purse and bra respectively, to stuff a ten dollar "donation" into the chest pocket of the frayed sports coat he was wearing.

"Awright now, y'all be careful out there. Don't get caught with yo' panties down."

They giggled their way into the liquor store. I just stood there not sure of where I was supposed to be at that particular moment. Rufus allowed me to stew-think for a few minutes before he explained, in a dismissive way.

"They're young hoes. Don't know nothing. Ain't never been nowhere. I'll give them a lil' conversation every now and then. And they'll give me a few coins. I think it's a fair exchange."

"So, you're pimping them?"

He seemed to go into a trance or something about my question. Finally, he responded.

"I suppose you could say that, if you were looking at it from your warped point of view."

I had to push back – "What would you call it?"

"I would call it, maybe, 'Rufus # 101' to two young ignorant ass hoes. They showed up with a couple of their girlfriends some time ago, to be 'Rufused', but I 'Rufused' because I didn't want to be bothered. They wanted somebody to pimp them, and I didn't want to be sucked into that, too much work."

The brother had me by the short hairs again. I didn't know whether to shit or go blind.

"Rufus, look, you're confusing me. Why would you refuse to be sucked into somebody giving you money?"

Brother had to shake his head like a dog shaking off water, trying to be transparent with me.

"Look, I just told you, it's too much work. I would be reduced to the level of a factory worker, one of those Charlie Chaplin caricatures, if I allowed myself to be seduced into conveying belt pussy."

Did I hear him say "Charlie Chaplin?" one of my idols? Did I hear from him say what he just said?

"Rufus, did I hear you say what I just heard you say?"

"What was that, champ?"

"You just used Charlie Chaplin to suggest what would be bad about pimping."

"Oh, did I do that? Excuse me, Willie, I have to have a lil' talk with this brother."

❦

Tuesday afternoon in front of the ocean, or as he called it "Yemanya."

"Rufus, what's so 'ye-ma-ya' about the ocean?"

I'll never be able to forget how incredibly he handled my ignorance. He did it quietly and patiently.

"Willie, you see this ocean, all of what is spread out in front of us?"

"I see it, I see it."

"Then you won't have any problem understanding that we all came from this, from this ocean. Had enough 'Origin of the Species' stuff to follow me?"

I nodded yes, wishing that I had a beer to carry me past his rap.

"I'm not going to take you past what I know, but let me say this. Come to the ocean as often as you can."

"To have rituals and stuff?"

"No sir, not to have rituals and stuff, but to acknowledge your Mother."

"Why do you say 'Mother'."

"Hey, look, man, what do you think your mother's amniotic fluid represents? What it is! Every woman on this planet is a Yemanya – dig it? Different people pronounce the words different ways, but it all symbolizes the same thing – women are the Birthers of our planet. Dig it?

If we didn't have women on the planet, we wouldn't have Beings. That's all I got to say on that."

We must've spent another hour on the Long Beach beach front, mostly staring at each other and the ocean.

I kept flash backing to the time I had spent on the ocean front with ZiZi, just a day ago, only a few hours ago.

"So, there, that was the deal they offered me."

"Huh?"

"Come on back, Willie. You didn't hear a word I said, did you?"

I guess the blank expression on my face said everything.

"Missing her already, huh?"

He sounded very sympathetic, unusually gentle. I decided to deflect the conversation.

"So, what happened to you over the weekend? We were going to hook up with you."

He leaned over and started sifting sand thru his fingers, just a little boy at the beach.

"I spent the weekend at the V.A."

I gave him a little space. I didn't want to probe, to make him feel that I was trying to get up into his bidness.

"Anything serious?"

"I was feeling suicidal, so they invited me to come in and talk about it."

I had to look at him real hard to make sure he wasn't doing a Rufus on me. This was real.

"Anything I can do?" I felt kind of stupid, asking a question like that, but I just couldn't help myself.

"Yeah, that's what the doctor told me when I told him that I had been talking to you about this stuff you're writing. I told him that me talking to you about the 'Nam had triggered this suicide stuff.

We had a long talk. He even made it possible for me to participate in a group thing on the weekend. I think that helped me a lot, just being with a bunch of people who had a lot in common."

"Did they give you any medicines? Something to chill you out?"

"Yeahhh, they always send me down to the pharmacy at the end of the day, but I won't take any of that chemical crap. I'll pick it up, just to have it on my record, but I won't take it. I usually give to somebody who wants it."

"So, what did the doctor say about you talking to me. You say it triggered …?"

"He advised me to keep on talking, he said, 'It may un-constipate you, psychologically'. These young shrinks really know how to lay it out."

"Well, that's good news. When do you want to get back on the track?"

"I'm on the track, that's what I was trying to talk to you, but you had your head in San Francisco…"

"Sorry, Rufus, I guess you caught me red handed."

"Ain't no real big thang. I was just trying to tell you about how I was railroaded into becoming a 'tunnel rat'."

"A 'tunnel rat'? What's that?"

"Let me tell you what it was…"

CHAPTER 7

"It was crystal clear to me and everybody else that there was some deep shit brewing between me and the 1ˢᵗ Sergeant."

"This is the one who talked about you being a gangsta from Chicago?"

"You got that right. The dirtyrottensnakedogfacist – barbarian snakedogasshole!"

Rufus didn't use an excessive amount of profanity, but he did have a unique way of stringing words together about people he didn't like.

"It was brewing, not just between me and this cracker dog but the whole machine. I had gotten myself a couple Article 15's, been almost framed into a 'negligence of duty' rap by being caught asleep on guard duty. Just little shit, but it was beginning to turd up.

This is the way things were waading up when I got called into the Captain's office. The 1ˢᵗ Sergeant was there and this guy from the Australian Army's School of Military Engineering. The way Captain Bonebrake explained it was real simple.

'Private, it looks like you're closing in on a three-year stay in the slammer. However, our Australian friend here may be able to save your ass. Major Knights Bridge?'

The way this major explained it to me, I could barely understand a word he said, I could go to jail for three years. Or I could go with him and become a 'tunnel rat'. Of course, I chose to become a 'tunnel rat'. Who in the gawd awful hell wants to spend any time in jail? And then come out and have to make up for lost time?"

"I still don't know what a 'tunnel rat' is?"

"You will. Be right back, gotta go pee."

54

I had to smile, watching him limp –jog across the sand-stretch to the men's. He was such a tough little prick. Five-three or four, one hundred and ten, if that, all wire and ligaments; someone once described someone who looked like him. A real bantam weight.

"Awright now, got that done. You don't have to pee a lot, huh?"

"I go when I have to."

He did his familiar snarky frown. It said so much. O, so you think you're hot shit, huh?

"Where was I?"

"You were going to tell me what a tunnel rat is?"

"Well, I guess I'll have to use the past tense, you know, like what a tunnel rat was."

"Whatever." I was interested and anxious to hear what he had to say.

"O.k., so here's what happened. I was transferred to Major Knights Bridge's Australian Army School of Military Engineering, which meant that I was going to be sent to some place in Australia. That sounded damned good to me, to be away from Viet Nam.

Truth be told I had to go to the map to find out where Australia was located. Awright, it's this big ol' island over there. I was transported, lickety split, to this training facility, about 20 miles west of Sydney. Somebody gave us an 'orientation' talk/speech in this Australian language, that I could barely understand.

Crazy thing about the Australians. I could never really understand why they were in 'Nam, fighting on the American side. And they were serious about stuff. The Australians took care maximum bidness.

Personally, I was freaked out when one of these 'orientation' people started it running down what we were going to be doing. We, was a twenty-man group culled from the Americans. No, I don't mean that there were 25 Americans as a group. We really had a diverse group of 'crazies', which is what I grew to call us.

There were a bunch of 'Hispanics' (this included some Puerto Ricans who said, 'we Hispanics') a collection of 'Gringos' (guys from the West Virginia coal mines, who were used to working underground, in coal mines) and me, yours truly. We were pushed into a three-month intensive, intensive training program. Understand 'intensive, intensive', Willie? Including extra pay."

"I'm sure I will, once you finish explaining it."

He shook his head back 'n forth, like somebody trying to get rid of a bad idea.

"I'm watching you, Willie; I got my eye on you. You're like one of those shrinks that try to tell you what they're thinking about, by asking you what you think."

I sensed that we were about to wander off into some kind of psycho thing that I wasn't prepared to deal with, so I decided to push back, hard.

"Rufus, look, I'm trying to put the shit together to write the best book that's ever been written, concerning a Viet Nam vet, all the way up to Trump shit. Dig it?"

Sitting right next to me on the beach at Long Beach, the brother broke it down. He started dishing, like nothing had ever been said, about what he had just said.

"We were called 'combat engineers'. A three-month course. Mine detection, booby trap disarming, tunnel searching – right; tunnel rats. I came off this shit feeling like I had had the secrets of the enemy revealed to me. That was the way it was. Dig?"

All I had to do was nod, to spur him on.

"What I'm trying to say is that I had no idea what I was going to be asked to do, until we **Did it**. Can you image somebody asking you, telling you to go down into a hole to kill somebody? That's what it was all about, basically.

Got to give it to these Aussies, that's what we called 'em, after we got to know 'em a little bit. They really knew their shit.

I don't know where they got this fancy title – 'Australia Army School of Engineering' from. But that's what they called it. A three-month session to learn how to go down into the Viet Cong's tunnels. These were some really smart ass people. They had started building those tunnels when the French were in control.

You hear what I'm saying, Willie?"

I nodded yes, yes, yes. I hear what you're saying. His eyes were starting to sparkle and he was using more gestures than usual.

"They had hospitals. Hospitals! Store houses, arsenals, cities underground. Our job, the 'tunnel rats', was to go down into these places and cause as much damage as possible, which meant killing as many people as you could find. And picking up, intel info, etc., etc., etc.

I almost opted out because I saw us as suicide victims. I mean, what chance did we have of going down into one of these holes and coming out alive? And the other stuff we were trained to do, above ground, was just as dangerous – mine detection, booby trap disarming, demolitions. Aside from everything else, I had a little taste of claustrophobia in my system.

Major Knights Bridge laid it on the line to me."

"See heah, Private Dixon. The American army wants to sentence you to a few years in the slammer, as Captain Bonebrake calls it. Now then, after you serve your years in the 'slammer', you will be required to make up the time you've missed. In a sense, your interest will take quite a time to catch up with your principal.

Are you getting me, Private Dixon?"

"'Yessir!' What else could I say? He had my balls in a bucket."

"Very good Private. I think, if you come out of this in one piece, you'll be considered a hero. You are dismissed, Private."

"So, that's how I became a tunnel rat. But there was other stuff happening too. While I was going thru this tunnel rat training all week, I was going into Sydney, about 20 miles west of us. Now you have to remember, I had been plucked right out of the Viet Nam jungles to be in this unit in Australia.

Australia was very different from 'Nam, very different. A big ol' hot place where people drank a lot of beer. That's what these guys in my unit wanted to do on the weekend, every weekend. We worked our asses off five days a week and come Friday night, it was Sydney and beer. Sydney, that's where I met Yvonne Goolagong."

He paused to sift the sand thru his fingers, a very contemplative gesture. He made me think of someone, a Muslim or maybe a Catholic, doing his prayer beads.

"Yvonne was working as a checkout clerk in the local super market. I'll never be able to remember why I went into this market. One thing I do know is that I couldn't hang out with those beer drinking Aussies.

Hardly anybody in the market when I went in there, a rare thing on a Friday evening. I think I bought a few apples or something. Maybe I was doing something to get away from the beer drinkers.

I placed the apples on the counter and we looked up into each other's eyes. It was really and truly love at first sight, on my side. She told me what the price of the apples were, I paid her and stood there, looking at her like a fool.

'Anything else for you today, sah?'

I could barely nod my head – 'No, no, no'. She sounded like an angel. She had this soft, low, sweet voice. I was double hooked. I loved the way she looked. And then she had this voice ....."

"I hear what you're saying, that was one of the things that drew me into ZiZi."

"This your lady from up north?"

"Yes, but go on, I want to hear this."

Funny, when I think back on it, how the beach and the ocean ("Yemanya") seemed to tighten around us, to become more intimate, in a manner of speaking.

"Yvonne was an Aboriginal. You know what that is, Willie?"

"One of the people who were in Australia when the White folks showed up."

"Give that man the kewpie doll! You got that exactly right! I had seen these people in different places around, but I had never been close to one, and I had never thought about falling in love with one of them.

I had to buy apples for three weekends before she would agree to take a walk around the block with me."

"I would like to take a walk with you, but my parents want to meet you first."

"What was she? Eighteen? Nineteen? Where I came from girls in their late teens were damned near considered women. They definitely didn't have to ask their parents for permission to walk around the block with somebody. Well, what the hell, when in Australia, do what the Australians do. She got off work, I met her in front of the store at 8:30 p.m. and we started walking. And walking. And walking. I was in damned good shape, so the walking was not a problem, but where in the hell were we walking to?

I have to admit that I was beginning to feel a bit skittish when we wound up in this shanty town. A real shanty town, Willie, not a slum like we have on the Westside and the Southside of Chicago."

"I've seen pictures, read articles about the situation in National Geographic. Rufus, I have an idea. Why don't we continue this at the Salamat Po, I'm feeling kinda snackish."

"That sounds like a rational idea, Willie, quite rational." He spoke like a real Aussie.

🔥

Brother Rufus must've been feeling snackish himself, judging from the way he attacked this chicken adobo Lola placed in front of him.

"So, what's happenin' with your cat? With Tarzan?"

"Awww, that rascal. He's too much. He's been bringing this black 'n white beauty around. I call her Jane, you know, like Tarzan and Jane?"

"I'm hip to 'em."

"But I've been running them off the premises. I don't think Mr. Kim wants to see a cat colony in his backyard."

We had a quiet little chuckle about that. It was time for a piece of cassava cake, a cup of tea and the rest of the story about him and Yvonne Goolagong.

"So, what happened then?"

"What happened about what?"

Brother was playing one of his little games with me. He was such a joker.

"About you and Ms. Goolagong, her parents?"

"Willie, I got to give it to you, you are a persistent cat. You're not related to Tarzan, are you?"

"Is he Black?"

I think it was the first time I had scored a real down to earth belly laugh out of Rufus. People actually turned around with smiles on their faces. It was that kind of laugh.

"You know something, Willie, he's pure black all the way."

"Ms. Goolagong?"

He turned serious immediately, took a sip of his tea and got back into his story.

"We took the walk, a number of walks, after I had satisfied Mr. and Mrs. Goolagong that I was not going to mistreat their daughter in any way.

Yvonne was, in a sense, all they had. You know, you hear words like 'grinding poverty' or you read words like that and they don't really mean anything until you experience, get up close to it.

Father Goolagong and Mother Goolagong had come from the 'Outback', that's what they called it, with nothing but the dirty, raggedy clothes on their backs. The whole shanty town was like that. And despite all of it, they were proud people.

It was hard for me to wrap my head around their proud thing. They looked like they were starving to death. And like I said, they were dirty and raggedy. But there was a way that the Father, sat on the dirt floor of their shanty and talked to me like a proper Dad would talk to any young dude who was obviously interested in trying to get into his daughter's panties."

"What did he say to you?"

"Well, he didn't give me permission to walk his daughter home from her job on this particular Friday night. Or to be anywhere near her 'til after my third visit. Basically, I just bribed my way into the family circle. The Father smoked cigarettes, so I followed Yvonne home, walking a hundred yards behind her in the dark, with a carton of cigarettes and a sack full of canned goods, a dozen apples.

Yvonne knew what I was doing when she sold me this stuff, and she was really pleased, I could tell.

So, that's how it started. I would trip into town on Friday night, buy a bunch of groceries and follow Yvonne home. After my third visit, Father said; 'You are a serious young man. You may walk with Yvonne, but no tricky stuff. You understand me?'

'Yessir'. I would've agreed to anything. Yvonne had my nose opened so wide you could've driven a Mack truck thru it."

"O yeahhh, I know what it's like to have your nose open."

We shared a brother to brother laugh on that one.

"Let me add this. It didn't take long for word to get around, about me and Yvonne, amongst the guys in my unit, or as the Aussies called us – 'mites', meaning 'mates'. Being the kind of heartless, immoral little beasties we were, I thought I would get some kind of flak from my 'mites', 'specially from the Aussies. But that wasn't the way it went down.

Just before I was on my way to meet Yvonne on this particular Friday evening, I get a call from Major Knights Bridge's office. Awww shit, now what? What did I do? Are they going to take my weekend pass away? Are they going to keep me away from Yvonne?

'Private Dixon reporting as ordered. Sir.'

Knights Bridge was real ol' school British Army, totally driven by the Code.

'Private Dixon, I have information that you have been seeing one of the local maidens. Is that correct?'

'Uhh, well, uhh, yessir.'

'Will you be seeing that young lady this evening?'

'Yessir, as soon as she gets off from work.'

'Very good, Private. I've arranged for you to have transport to the young lady's place of employment and then to her home. That is all, Private.'

I had dropped my jaw down to my shoe tops. What? What did this mean?

'Uhh, yessir, thank you, sir.'

He mumbled under his breath as I stumbled out of his office... It's a bloody damned shame the way these people are being treated. They've done nothing to deserve being treated like animals.

I can't begin to tell you how I felt when I looked up at this deuce and a half, fully loaded and packed with all kinds of stuff: clothes, shoes, cigarettes, candy, can goods, books, yes, even beer.

Yvonne, who was usually cool about stuff, looked like she was gonna faint when this truck, expertly driven by one of my 'mites', pulled up in front of her workplace.

'Melvin, what's this?'

'Get in.'

It seemed like everybody in my unit had contributed. And the word spread like an Australian wildfire. By the time we got to the Goolagong shanty town, everybody knew everything. 'The Yank', that's what they called me. 'The Yank' was bringing goodies to the Goolagong estate.

It took a few minutes of patient explanation for Yvonne to explain to her Mother and Father that I was giving all of this stuff to them. Yvonne explained to me that they thought I was giving them all of these goodies for their daughter. I hadn't even thought about anything like that."

"They thought you were bringing them a dowry."

"Damn, Willie, you know every damned thing, don't you?"

"Well, not everything."

"Well, you got it right. The funny thing that happened, I noticed, is that we were unloading stuff thru the front door, stacking it in the back room and Father Goolagong was giving stuff away out of the back door. I couldn't get with that. I asked Yvonne to run it down to me. I'm not going to try to talk the way they talked, the way she talked. I could never get beyond 'mite'."

"I hear you, Rufus, I hear you."

"She said, it's like this, Mel, if my Dad has so much and our mites have so little, that would mean, pardon me French, that my Dad, our family are a bunch of greedy bastards."

'Dig what she was saying to me, Willie?'

I had a very clear idea of what he was saying. That she had said to him, but I didn't want to shortchange his explanation.

"I'm not quite sure what she was saying, Rufus, maybe you can, uhhh, break it down to me."

He gave me his usual multi-landscaped snarky look. C'mon, man, you trying to mess with me or what? Before he got into it, I signaled to Lola for another pot of Oolong tea and a couple more cassava cookies.

"What it meant was that the Aboriginal people, Yvonne's people had discovered, early on, how rotten Capitalism could be, if it was mis-used. Dig it?"

It was time for me to stop acting like I was "cute", that I knew everything. It was time to put on the knee pads.

"Rufus, to be honest with you, I can't really say that I know what you're talking about."

"Glad to hear you say that, champ. It gives me a chance to explain what I didn't have a grip on either, way back then. What Yvonne explained to me was this; her family had come into a lot, suddenly. Now, they could suddenly declare themselves 'rich' whatever that meant. Or they could share whatever they had come into, which would make everybody feel better because it would mean that each one had to share in the good fortune."

I leaped out at him because I had studied Communism, Capitalism, a whole bunch of these issues in college.

"So, they were communists? That's what you're saying, huh?"

"Sorry, Willie, that ain't what I'm saying, what was explained to me. Yvonne, who usually had a somewhat cheerful looking face, turned purple dark on me as she explained... 'Melvin, listen to me close, o.k. because I may not be able to explain this more than once.

We, the people they call Aboriginals, have been inside this land for forty thousand years. Our Elders count better and say that our Dream Time pre-dates the European years. We may be the ones who came before those who came before those who came before those who came before those who came before.

And then the others came. We had no way of understanding where they came from. Who in the hell knew where this little English place was? This England they came from. We didn't have a clear idea of where they came from, but we've always known where we came from, our Dream Time tells us that ....'"

"They're deep people, deep people."

"You got that right, Uncle Willie, you got that right. So, she explains to me, 'We never picked up on the idea of being addicted to stuff, to 'wealth', to money, to one group of people having 'more' than the other group.

This was something that the invaders could never figure out about us. They thought we were 'poor' because we didn't feel the need to surround our lives with a lot of stuff. Believe me, when the invaders came we had everything we needed or wanted.

We only became poor when the invaders started stuffing us full of their poisonous ideas.'"

"Wowwww, that's what she said?"

"She said a whole lot more than that, but I can't remember all of it. Look why don't we get back at this tomorrow, I'm feeling sleepy."

"Late night last night?"

"Yeah, I guess you could say that. I tried going to sleep about 10:30, but I kept having these nightmares every time I dozed off. I don't know if it's from these pills they gave me at the V.A. or if it's just from this PTSD shit."

I paid the check, leaving my usual big tip.

"Have a good evening," Lola said as she ushered us out into the evening. Time to mask back up, keep that distance.

"Give you a lift, Rufus?"

"Naw, I'm cool. What would Tarzan think seeing me wheel up."

"Tomorrow? Same time?"

He nodded yes and limp-strutted away.

CHAPTER 8

"So, then what happened?"

"Well, that's how it ended, this time. ZiZi, are you crying?"

"Well, not exactly. I'm trying not to. You're telling me the story of a man who had love, who fell in love with an Australian woman?"

"An Aboriginal woman. There's a big difference."

"Educate me, I don't know a whole lot about Australia."

"I don't know a whole lot myself, but I'm learning."

"This happened fifty some years ago and it sounds like something that happened yesterday."

"That's the feeling I have, the vibe I'm trying to bring to the story as I make my outline, put the notes together about the whole scene. So, that's that, now then, concerning our business…"

"I'll be moving to Long Beach right after Nov. 3rd."

"Right after Biden-Harris Kicks that barbarian's ass out into the streets."

"My goodness, sir, such language!"

Forty-five minutes later after a lot of gorgeous language had been exchanged; it was time for another long night without my ZiZi. I got back to my outline of "Rufus's story".

NEXT DAY

I almost panicked when I pulled into the mall parking lot and didn't see Rufus in his usual spot. I parked and studied my watch. Two p.m.

He was supposed to be in his spot now. I just sat there, drumming on the steering wheel, feeling a little frustrated. Where was this guy? I was deep into his story, I wanted more of it.

I did a double take – Rufus strolling out of the liquor store. What the hell was he doing in the liquor store? A non-drinker.

"Hey Rufus!" I called out to him. The liquor store parking lot regulars were surreptitiously passing a half gallon jug of cheap wine around and, as usual, having an animated discussion – argument about something.

"Hey Rufus!" I called out to him again. He did his little hip cripple-strut over to me.

"Who you shouting at Willie?! You think I can't hear? That I can't see?! What's happenin?"

Same ol' irascible rascal. He made me smile, just thinking about the way he was.

"Oh, nothing much. I was just getting ready to take a drive up to Griffith Park. You want to take a ride?"

What made me come up with something like that? He gave me a weird look, above the level of his mask. Never knew anybody who could say so much without saying a word. It was all in his eyes.

Or the way he slouched in place. Or the way he jammed his hands down into his pants pockets.

"Griffith Park, huh? I ain't been up there in years."

"Well?" I opened the passenger side door for him. He paused, just before sliding in to ask: "Uhh, how're we going to do social distancing?"

"Simple. Easy. You lean as far as you can in that direction, and I'll lean as far as I can in this direction. And we'll keep our masks on 'til we get to the park."

I'll never know why that struck his funny bone in such a funny way, but he laughed himself silly until we did the on ramp at Willow.

"Awright now, brother Willie, be careful. You know a lot of these idiots out here want to kill themselves, commit suicide because they've fallen in love with the Trumpster."

I parsed that around in my skull for a few miles, keeping the northbound truck brigade in cautious sight. I gave up after a bit, I couldn't figure out what he meant.

Tunnel Rat, Going Thru A Tunnel

I really grew to love the way he could be completely silent and then open up on you, like someone who wanted to pour his soul out to you. I could never figure out what triggered him, what turned him on.

"What's this?" He asked me as we twisted around this road leading up to the Planetarium."

Neil Degrasse Tyson Country

"I thought you said we were going to the park."

"The Planetarium is in the park, well, part of it."

He got a big laugh out of that, for some reason. In any case, there we were, "*on top of the world*," overlooking the Los Angeles Basin.

♨

We sat on a bench that gave us a clear view all the way up to Santa Monica. A beautifully clear day. He opened up without any pressure from me.

"My time was winding down, we had three more weekends in Sydney, in Australia, before being shipped back to Viet Nam as official 'tunnel rats'."

"I hate to say it, but that sounds like a terrible name, to stick on somebody."

"Well, what else would you call us? Tunnel rodents? Underground troops? People under soil? Tunnel rats were exactly the right name for us."

I had a few minutes of reluctance about wanting to hear this tunnel rat's story. I tried to deflect the story by trying to talk about other things. The day seemed too gorgeous to be talking about rat shit.

"Did I tell you I talked to ZiZi, my girl, about you last night?"

"I guess you don't want to hear about this ugly tunnel rat shit, huh?"

He had beaten me to the pass.

"I have to be honest with you, Rufus. In a way I don't want to hear about it. But, I have to hear about it or else I won't be able to write your story."

"Yeah, that's the way I feel too."

That's all he needed. This is what he told me, sitting high up there at the Planetarium, the Los Angeles Basin and the ocean sprawled out around us.

"I had two more weekends left on the calendar before we would be returning to Viet Nam, for me to begin my tunnel rat career."

Music drifted over to us from somebody's car radio.

"Wowww, Charlie Parker, 'Laura'. That's magic. I haven't heard that one in a hundred years."

"Yeah, 'Bird' was something else."

"You know about Charlie Parker, 'Bird'?"

"I'm happy to say, yes. I do. My Dad had a whole bunch of his stuff."

"Lucky you."

And then, there was that by now familiar space away look.

"So, you had two more weekends?"

"Yeah, two more weekends, before my return to Hell. I decided that I wanted Yvonne to be my wife, to get married before I started climbing down into the rat holes, the tunnels."

Rufus was constantly doing some kind of plot twist on my head. I was beginning to think about bringing a pen and a notebook to our meetings, but I immediately vetoed it because I felt it would inhibit our relationship. You know how it is with some people. The minute they see a tape recorder, or see you pull out a pad and pen, things go south.

"You decided to get married?"

"Yeahhh, I can't figure why, except for the fact that I was in love."

"You, in love?"

"What's the problem? You don't think that I could be in love?"

"Sorry, Rufus, you just come across as such a hard case at times."

"I am a hard case. But I wasn't always the way I am now. Back then, I guess you could've called me a sentimentalist, like Tarzan.

So, yeah, I asked Yvonne to marry me. And to my surprise she agreed. I leveled with her. I told her that what I was doing was very dangerous and that I might not come back. She brushed it all aside – 'you will be back'. That was all she said. And from that point, it was On!

Father and Mother Googalong gave us their blessings and started preparing a wedding party..."

"Two weekends ahead of time?"

"That's correcto, amigo. Now comes the big problem. Who do we get to say the words? To make the thing Real? I had an appointment with the Unit Chaplain that almost turned into a homicide."

'I'm sorry, Private,' he says to me, 'I won't have anything to do with the marriage of a heathen prostitute ....' That was as far as he got before I had run around the corner of his desk and grabbed his scrawny neck in this python choke hold. If one of my 'mites' had not been passing by the open door of his office, I would have killed that motherfucker!"

"Rufus, I've never heard you cuss before."

"Well, I don't usually. I don't like people who use profanity a lot, I think it's uncouth."

"Oh …" What else could I say?

"Yeahhh, I would've strangled this sleazy bastard if Rudy hadn't pulled my arms away from his neck. Of course, it was a big thing. Major Knights Bridge had me in his office within the hour, along with Chaplain Jones.

The Major didn't fool around. He was the judge, and jury. He listened carefully to Chaplain Jones lie about being attacked first."

'Sah, this man came into my office and attacked me without any provocation whatsoever.'

'Now, why do you think he did that, Chaplain Jones?'

'Sah, I don't have the foggiest, sah.'

"It seemed like I was going to be railroaded. What justice could I expect to receive? A couple ol' school, upper crusted English officers talking to each other."

'Now then, Private Dixon, leave us hear your side of the story.'

"I told it plain 'n simple, including the part about losing my temper and trying to strangle the Chaplain. At the end of my story, the Major turned to the Chaplain and asked, in this real soft, dangerous sounding voice – 'Chaplain Jones, is this true? What Private has just said? That you called his fiancée a prostitute? Do you know, for a fact that Private Dixon's fiancée is a prostitute?'"

"The Chaplain's head was drooping down between his legs like a whipped dog. The Major was not finished with him."

'Answer my question Chaplain!' The Major slammed his command stick on his desk and his face turned brick red.

'No sah, I cawn't say for a fact that Private Dixon's fiancée is a prostitute.'

'Then why in hell did you say that?!'

"The Major was not very tall, but when he stood up behind his desk, he looked about 7 feet tall. The Chaplain looked like he was going to cry. I didn't feel sorry for him. The office was completely quiet for a few minutes. Major Knights Bridge leaned across his desk on his knuckles."

'Chaplain Jones, your 'services' are no longer required in this unit. As a matter of fact, I shall see to it that your 'services' will no longer be required in the Army. Are you getting me, Jones?'

"The scene was so cold. The Major was turning him out, right then and there."

'You are dismissed, Jones.' Jones stood and tried to salute, but the Major wouldn't let him – 'I do not return salutes by racists, Jones.' That was all he said. And Jones slithered out.

'Now, back to you, Private Dixon. Leave the date, the time and place where your wedding is scheduled to take place and we will have a proper chaplain on hand to perform the rites. That will be all, Private.'

'Thank you, sah.'

He almost smiled as he returned my salute.

❦

"We had a great wedding. I didn't know a whole lot about Aborigine customs and all of that, but I soon found out, by the time we went into the second day of our marriage. I can definitely say that I knew a whole lot more than I already knew.

I had the impression, like a lot of other people, that the Aboriginal people were kind of solemn, you know, not too much into partay. I had to back off of that. These were people who had a great sense of humor, kinda bawdy too, if you know what I mean?

I must've had a hundred jokes translated to me about what my virgin bride was going to do to me on our honeymoon. Jokes about magic herbs I could take to 'defend' myself. And then we danced. And danced. And danced. 'Till dawn. And then we danced some more.

I was beginning to think that I would never have a private time with Yvonne, with my bride. But then, the moment came, and we were off. Did I mention that Major Knights Bridge and most of the members of my unit came to the wedding?"

"Sounds like the Major was really a righteous dude."

"You're right on the button, Willie boy, he was a righteous dude. I'll tell you more about him as we get into this. Yeah, it was a great wedding, but it didn't come close to the night we spent out in the bush, buck nekkid, loving each other.

We didn't have an opportunity to do that but a few times, to be buck nekkid in the moonlight, before my time to return to Hell came."

"That sudden, huh?"

"Yeah, about that sudden. Hey, uhh, you had anything to eat lately? I see a Sub over there. Can you dig a Sub, or are you one of those veggie villains?"

"Gimme a break, Rufus, you know I eat meat. Let's get something."

I really liked the way this little brother went about things. He could've been starving to death, but he would never ask you to feed him, he would suggest that we have something to eat. I didn't mind his way of going about things at all. I felt that I was receiving much more than I was giving.

We took our sandwiches back to the bench and sat there, snacking. As I look back on the scene, I felt that there was something almost cosmic happening. Maybe it's the writer in me, but I couldn't help feeling the cosmic thing. There we were, at the Planetarium, nestled against the sky, if you wanted to get poetic about it.

A truly insane man was doing everything possible to try to get a second chance to destroy America, not a democracy, as a lot of people claimed it to be, but America, the country. He was tripping around the country, trying to whip up hate, discord, and madness.

And he had convinced millions of White people (and some weirdass 'others') to join his campaigns. I clearly understood why millions of White folks were in the MAGA camp. They wanted to retain a privileged place in our society, even those who weren't racists. My problem was with the people of color who had joined the Make America White (oops) Great Again Movement.

Certainly, there weren't millions of Black, Brown and Asians strolling around with AKAs strapped on their minds, but there were enough to be visible.

Why would any African-American support a Trump, after a brief, casual review of some of his racist stances, rants? – 'Lynch, the Central Park Five!' 'Obama wasn't born in America.' 'I've done more for African-Americans than any president since Abraham Lincoln.'

Obviously, that explained the ultra-high percentage of African-American Covid19 deaths, the unemployment rates in African-American communities, the ongoing African-American struggle to avoid being murdered by police in the street or unjustly treated by the so called '*Justice System*'. Why wouldn't we vote for him as though we had nothing to lose?

And why wouldn't Latino voters flock to the banner of the racist asshole who snatched babies out of their mother's arms, who made hundreds, if not thousands of children permanently displaced people, who locked up others in cages and called their fathers, sons, uncles, brothers, drug dealers and rapists?

Asians, the Chinese mostly, were guilty of releasing the "Chinese virus" on his precious White people. That was his lie-line, despite the fact that the virus was proven to have been imported from Europe.

Rufus had excellent perception, superior timing.

"Being up here gives a man a lot to think about, huh?"

He didn't interrupt my thoughts, he blended in. We took simultaneous sips of our oversized Cokes. I nodded in agreement. It was time to get back on the track, the sun was slowly settling behind the Pacific Ocean.

CHAPTER 9

"Bam! It was like that. We dismount the calm, peaceful horse we had ridden in on from Australia and the next day we were on this buckin' bronc called the Vietnamese battlefield, the jungle."

"I like that, Rufus, I like that, it's a helluva an analogy...."

"Well, I don't care whether you like it or not, that's what it felt like to me."

Yep, we were back on track. I could never figure out when or where his hostility would flare up. I just had to go with the flow.

"Remember now, I'm in the American Military, but I'm attached to this Australia unit called the Australian Army School of Engineering. I could never figure why they called it that, but that wasn't my job. I found out what my job was the second day we were in the field.

Truth be told, I cannot, for the life of me, remember why we were walking thru this jungle. A small squad, maybe twenty people, I was one of the designated booby trap finders.

Me and this little stringy Aussie guy. I call him that because that's what he looked like, a bundle of strings with some flesh hanging on. Somebody up front whispered 'booby'. This was for me and 'Mr. Strings' to move up in front of the squad, to check for booby traps.

I had been trained very well, but 'Mr. Strings' had the experience. We moved ahead and did it all by pantomime from that point on. He pointed at a round patch of soil on the path in front of us. I studied the patch of soil and I could see what he was showing me. The patch of soil was a different color than the rest of the soil. Freshly planted land mines, teacup sized mines that could blow off your big toe or your foot. They were activated by pressure, like pressing on a light switch. Me and 'Mr. Strings' got busy and deactivated a small mine field planted on this path. About fifteen mines. Probe with your knife, dig the bad boy out very, very carefully and detach this trip spring.

I was soaking with sweat from nervous tension by the time 'Mr Strings' announced; 'looks good to go now.' We signaled for the squad to move forward. It would be impossible to describe how I felt, the pride I felt, as these guys walked on this path that me and 'Mr. Strings' had cleared for them.

'Good show, Mel, good show,' a few of them mumbled as they walked past. Others patted me on the back and smiled. I had saved somebody's foot from being blown off. Or maybe I had saved a life. I felt humble and proud. That was just the beginning.

Working with 'Mr. Strings' was an incredible experience. This little funny talking dude (funny to me) was like a jungle Sherlock Holmes. He could read the ground. He could tell what had passed thru a certain section by the way the leaves had been twisted. He saved my ass at least a dozen times.

'Don't touch that, mite — it will pull that platform full of spikes down on yer' end.'

Punji sticks, 'seasoned' by human and animal shit, guaranteed to cause blood poison. Defusing weirdly made bombs, designed to blow five ten seconds after you picked them up.

'That was close, another two seconds and we would be in Heaven now. Or wherever.'

'Mr. Strings' had something like a 6th sense about things. I asked him about how he had learned how to 'read' so well."

"Well, mite, it comes from my living with the Abo people."

"With the Aboriginal people?"

"That's what I just said."

I got an immediate glimpse of where Rufus had picked up some of his stuff.

"So, how did you come to hang out with the Aboriginals?"

"You know that my wife is an Aboriginal?"

"I didn't hang out, I lived with them for most of my growing up years."

"And I know your wife is an Aboriginal being with them."

"So, how did that come about?"

"Melvin, you do ask a lot of questions."

"Sorry, I'm just curious."

"No problem, mite, if you don't ask questions, you'll be going around pretending to know every bloody thing, just like everybody else. I'll just say this. I was abandoned when I was about four – five. Me Mum was a young girl who got herself knocked up by this rich kid on this sheep ranch. Anyway, let's skip the sentimental part. I thought I was an Abo 'til I was about fifteen or so. They had adopted me.

That's when some bloody blokes come along, discovered I was a White and took me away.

'You can't live out 'ere with these Black fellas' they called us, then, and took me to a bloody orphanage in the city. Of course, I ran away from the orphanage after a couple years and hung out, as you Yanks say it. The minute I turned 18 I joined up. I been in for four years now and it looks like this is where I'm gonna spend the rest of me life, unless I get my arse blown off by one of these devices."

A really spectacular sunset -- fiery orange, shades of green, corn silk yellow, reddish tinges.

"Mr. Strings sounds like an interesting character."

"He was, 'til he got his arse blown off."

This guy was constantly doing plot twists on my head. Damn, I wasn't prepared to hear that. Rufus seemed to ignore the shocked look on my face.

"That was the way it went, the way stuff happened. But before 'he got is arse blown off,' we went into about a dozen tunnels together. The first time I slipped thru a tunnel opening I was shaking like a leaf. My teeth were chattering. I peed on myself, but I didn't notice it because of the nervous sweat that poured off my body.

'Mr. Strings' had given me some good advice about a number of things … 'don't take that bloody .45, if you have to fire the bloody thing in a close space, you'll be deaf for a time. And you can't afford to be deaf down there. You need to be able to hear everything, all the time, your life depends on it.'

We, me and 'Mr. Strings' got the call on a Friday morning. Never will forget it. The sergeant in charge gave us a briefing.

'We're going to be forward, but it looks like the Viet Cong have established a small complex in this area. We can't afford to bypass it because we'll have these little buggers bitin' us in the arse later.'

A small complex. That could mean that they had a small village dug underground, with a hundred people or more. A small complex might mean that they had a communications system set up that passed info about troop movements. A small complex could mean that ten booby trap people were down there designing spike balls or whatever.

Our job, me and 'Mr. Strings', was to go thru this hidden door, down into the *UNKNOWN*, and bring back all the intelligence we could find; maps stuff like that. And kill as many people as possible.

"The killing is going to be necessary, mite. You can't go down in there thinking about brotherhood and friendliness. You're invading their 'home' and they will kill you for doing that. If you don't kill them first."

"Hard to explain how strange/weird that sounded to me the first time I heard it … kill or be killed. And this other thing 'Mr. Strings' said more than once.

'I have a pill or two that you might want to keep with you, just in case you need to kill yourself. Or you might want to remember to save the last bullet for yourself. You do not want to be captured by these blokes, under any circumstances.'

There, there it was, the terrible circumstances."

The lights brightening up from the L.A. Basin suddenly seemed spooky, as though they were accentuating Rufus's tunnel story.

"I found out, along the way, that the Viet Cong had captured a tunnel rat, skinned the whole top half of his body and sent him back up to his unit. Fortunately, he died two days later."

"How could anybody do something that evil? I asked 'Mr. Strings'."

'It ain't evil, mite, they're just doing what they think they have to do to gain control of their ancestral land.'"

"Why don't they go about it in a civil way? The way we're trying to get equal rights in America?"

"'Mr. Strings' gave me his 'you're-an-idiot-look'."

"Mel, ol' boy, listen to me. These people, those Viet Namese broke away from China, centuries ago; the Chinese punished them horribly for being so arrogant. The Viet Namese struck. They kicked the Chinese out of Viet Nam by doing more horrible shit than the Chinese could think of doing. And the Chinese backed off. The Viet Namese had learned a lesson. If we're going to have to defend ourselves, then it's all in."

"Just think about it, mite; if you, your people in the U.S., were willing to do half of what these people here are willing to do, to be free, then you would've been free a long time ago."

"He actually said that?"

Rufus shot one of his snarky looks in my general direction.

"You think I'm lying to you?"

"No, I didn't mean that you were lying, it just seems like an unusual thing for an Australian, a soldier, to be talking like that."

"I know, I know." Rufus's expression went from snarky to sentimental. The brother was a stone-cold emotional chameleon.

"'Mr. Strings' said a lot of unusual stuff. For example, he didn't believe in war. 'War,' he said, 'serves only two purposes. It makes the rich richer and kills off a lot of poor people.'"

"So, I felt compelled to ask him, "Where do you fit in here, in all of this?"

"I don't fit in nowhere, mite, nowhere at all. That's why we're going into the unknown."

Sitting there, listening to this brother talk about 'Mr. Strings', the Viet Nam he had experienced, I tried to flash back to a movie, a play, a book about Viet Nam that had laid out this kind of nihilistic p.o.v. on my head. Well, maybe it wasn't nihilistic, it was simply one tunnel rat's point of view.

"Man, you talk about a tunnel of horrors. The entrance was blue black black and we had to crawl after we were lowered into the entrance. 'Mr. Strings' was in first and whispered – 'don't fart. Smell goes a long way down 'ere.'

I couldn't tell whether he was joking or not. We had crawled about twenty yards in the blue black before I heard a weird kind of scruffy sound come from 'Mr. Strings' crawling in front of me. What was that? What was happening?

'Snakes, I got 'em,' 'Strings' whispered back over his shoulder to me. Snakes? What the hell was he talking about? I found out later. A living booby trap."

"They had nailed a few snakes on the side of the tunnel. Actually, it was kind of a stupid thing to do because the snakes couldn't strike out like they usually do. So, all I had to do was slice their bloody 'eads off with me knife."

"'Mr. Strings' had supervised my arms equipment. I had a small pistol, either a Japanese Nambu, which looks like a baby German Luger, stuffed into my belt in back. I crawled with a .38 special revolver equipped with a silencer. Strictly non-standard. A razor-sharp knife (like 'Mr. Strings'), a flashlight and two grenades. No shirt and sometimes, no shoes. This first venture into the unknown, I had shoes on.

Hard to say how far we crawled, passing a whole herd of rats on my left side. I didn't flash my light on them because I could feel their paws gripping my fingers as they went past us in the tunnel.

How far did we crawl? Twenty miles? Ten miles? Of course it wasn't that far. But it seemed like it. Finally, I could see a glimmer of light thru 'Mr. Strings' legs in front of me. Somebody. Some people.

We crawled a few feet closer and I could see five men huddled over a table with a map on it, on the left corner of 'Mr. Strings' shoulder. It was so methodical, so matter of fact, that it seemed like the right thing to do. 'Mr. Strings' crawled out of the tunnel opening and shot three of the men in the head – 'don't do body, mite, go for the brains.'

And I shot the other two in the head. No one screamed or made any kind of outcry. They had been totally surprised and executed. We rolled up the map they had been studying and crawled back thru the tunnel."

It seemed like the whole world had changed, in just a few minutes. I was sitting next to a man who had killed people. It wasn't like he was bragging or anything. It was just a fact. I looked more closely at him."

"I have to ask, how did you feel?"

"...About killing?"

"Yes, about killing those people."

"I really didn't think about it 'til years later, years later. I was just doing a job I had been trained to do. Up 'til that time I had never been trained to do anything."

It was dark, but the Planetarium grounds were alive with people jogging around, walking around. We stood and just started walking around.

🌿

"We climbed in and out of a dozen tunnels together, over the course of about seven months, in between de-fusing ordinance, clearing booby traps. We were a good team. Our chemistry was so good, I think, because we were able to communicate so well with each other, without words.

It got to a point where I could just about feel what was happening with him, in the dark, and vice versa. We only used our flashlights, our torches, for what you might call 'emergencies.' Let me give you an example."

I never had a photographic memory or anything like that, but I never needed one with Rufus (formerly known as Melvin Montaigne Dixon, III) because the stuff he was laying on me was so graphic, so vivid.

"We're pretty far down into this tunnel, 'Mr. Strings' is in front, as the senior man, when 'Mr. Strings' says to me, just louder than a whisper' 'Mel, move up on me left 'ere and shoot this fuckin' thing. It's got me shoulder in 'is bleedin' mouth.'

I could not, for the life of me, figure out what he was talking about. But I trusted him completely. If he wanted me to crawl up on his left and shoot something, that's what I was going to do. And that's what I did. A strobe flash from my flashlight showed the whole thing. A fair-sized monkey had sank his canines into 'Mr. Strings's left shoulder. In the flash of my light, I caught the whole scene. This monkey, a trained tunnel keeper, had bit into 'Mr. Strings's shoulder and was not about to let go.

It's amazing to think back on it, about how calm we were, me and 'Mr. Strings'. We discussed how we should solve the problem in a few whispered sentences.'

Should I stab it to death?

'No, no don't stab. It might not let go if you stab. Shoot it thru the head, but don't hit me arm.'

I had one flash of my flashlight to show me where to aim. If I missed, the monkey's canines were still going to be embedded in 'Mr. Strings's shoulder. I got it right the first time. The monkey's brains splattered everywhere.

'Mr. Strings' pulled the monkey's head off of his shoulder and we continued our crawl thru the tunnel. The higher ups patted us on the head for giving them all of the maps, the intelligence material that we secured. But the big thing was the joke the Aussies made on 'Mr. Strings' after I told them about 'Mr. Strings' being bitten on the shoulder by a monkey.

'C'mon now, mite, tell us the truth. Were yer goin' down there for a rendezvous, or to get some info? Hah ha hah.'

It took me awhile to understand this 'gallows humor, Aussie style.' These guys could make fun of Death. That takes a lot of courage."

"Rufus, I have to be honest with you, I don't know whether to laugh or cry. You say 'Mr. Strings' got his arse blown off. How did that happen?"

I was asking questions and listening to his answers. But my mind was already focusing on the outline that I had going on. And the conversation I was going to have with ZiZi, if I got home before midnight.

"Why don't I tell you on the way back to Long Beach? Joe doesn't like to close up the liquor store 'til I'm on the scene."

"Joe? Mr. Kim?"

"Yeah, he's a good dude."

"How did that come about?"

"Damn, Willie West, you wanna know every damn thing."

"It's important for the, uhhh, for the story."

We stared at each other as we strolled to the car. The Storyteller and the Scribe. He was smiling at some secret joke. I was smiling at his smile.

"How did it happen? Well, I needed a place to pitch my tent and his back area looked like a good spot. How long ago? Last year, to be exact.

I didn't just plant myself on his ground, the way some dudes might've done. I went into the store and presented myself. I explained to him about my situation and all. And he gave me permission, simple as that. I guess I must've made a good impression on him."

"I get the impression that he's a good person."

"He is. He's a bidnessman, no doubt about it, but he's got a good heart. And he's kinda slick too. By letting me stay back there, it gives some people this idea that I'm some kind of guard or something. So, I guess it works out to everybody's advantage."

W

81

CHAPTER 10

"You asked me a little while ago about how I felt about killing people? Like I said, I didn't give it a lot of thought 'til years later. But I have to admit I did have regrets about a couple 'crawls' I made. The first one I made by myself, the second one was with 'Mr Strings'.

"Where was he when you did the first 'crawl'?"

"Sick. He had come down with a bad case of malaria. It was no real big thing, people got malaria all the time. The sergeant called on me and I went. To be frank with you, I was filled up to here with myself. I felt like I was incredible...."

"You mean – invincible."

"Yeah, that too. I located the entrance to this tunnel, and they lowered me down into it. By this time, I had figured a few things out. These tunnels were always humid as hell, so I went down with nothing on but my shorts and pants, but I was armed. I had my razor sharp, short bayonet attached to my belt and two pistols. One in my belt in back and I carried one in my hand.

I always felt like I was in another world, maybe outer space, or something, when I wormed my way thru these spaces. You had to be small to crawl thru because there was barely enough room to crouch in. They might've put sharpened bamboo stakes in the crawl space, nailed snakes to the wall, or positioned crazy ass monkeys to bite you, like what happened to 'Mr. Strings'.

I felt alive in a way I would never be able to explain. The hair on the back of my head felt like bristles on a cat's back. My nervous system was on high alert for anything, everything. I could hear a mouse piss on cotton from ten yards away."

"Really?!"

"Well, maybe not ten yards away, not that far, but I was really hyped, 'wired'."

We were stuck in a downtown traffic jam. Despite the pandemic there were still too many cars on the freeway. The screaming red ambulances bobbing and weaving thru the clinched cars, lights flashing, told us that there had been an accident ahead. Nothing to do but ooze along and listen to Rufus.

"The first sergeant had told me, confidentially; 'We think we may have one of the Biggies down there.'

I don't know why he told me that. It wouldn't've mattered whether they had Ho Chi Minh, or Baby Snooks down there, the danger would still be the same. I don't know how far I had crawled when I saw this dim, flickering light ahead of me, a bit off to the left.

Time to be ready for whatever. I inched along 'til I came to a room on my left, where the flickering light was coming from. I heard them before I peeked around the corner into the room. A man and a woman were on a futon, the woman mounted on the man's thighs, doing the nasty. The flickering light made sexy shadows on the ceiling.

I took a deep breath and exhaled slowly. I was really relieved to see them doing what they were doing. Number one, it meant that they were completely oblivious to me. Number two, doing what they were doing meant that they were alone, nobody else on the scene. I crept up behind the woman riding this man's thighs like a rocking chair and plunked off a round into the back of her head. That was the sound my pistol made with the silencer on it. Plunk.

She slumped down on his right shoulder, brains oozing out of her head. The man looked over her shoulder right into my face. He didn't scream or anything. He just looked me dead in the face and said, clear as day; 'Fuck you, American'.

I plunked him right between the eyes twice. That was the way it was, nothing personal. I saw that they had been drinking something. I took the bottle and started sipping as I looked around the space. Nothing that I could see that was of any value, no maps, stuff like that. Time to go.

I crawled back thru the tunnel, pausing to take a lil' sip from the bottle, from time to time. I don't know what it was. It tasted a little bit like moonshine and was strong. Strong. By the time they hauled me up thru the tunnel opening, I was semi-drunk."

"You said you had some regrets about what you did?"

"Yeah, I felt kinda bad about taking that couple's booze from them. I regretted that."

The traffic unclenched for us to make a faster ooze onto the 710 South.

Return to Long Beach

"The second regret happened during a crawl with 'Mr. Strings', fresh from his turn with malaria. He was still recovering from his monkey bite and malaria, but other than that he was good to go. It didn't take long for that to happen. We got the word and the instructions. And there we were, down there, in the Underworld.

Maybe I've said it before, but I'll say it again, being down there was like being in another world. I could call it 'the Underworld'. But it was more than that.

Willie, you ever thought of what it was like to be dead?"

I almost ran into the rear of one of these huge trucks that run up and down the 710. What it was like to be dead? Who in the hell ever thought about shit like that? All I could think of doing was shake my head. No No No. I shook my head No No No. And recognized a familiar pattern. We were about to be derailed, he was about to wander off, maybe detour from the subject.

"Rufus, I never thought about being dead, but that's what you were talking about."

"Hey, man, you don't have to remind me of what I was talking about! I know what I was talking about. Don't you remember?!"

I was hip to the game now, just stay focused and peaceful.

"Yeah, I remember. You were talking about your second moment of regret, during your tunnel rat days in Viet Nam..."

The traffic had jammed us again. The Port of Long Beach was doing big time bidness.

"Yeahhh, the second regret."

I glanced at him. He seemed to be doing a Method Actor number, doing a few deep breathing exercises, squeezing his eyes shut. I wondered about what was going to come out of all this.

"Awright, we're crawling thru the muddy water in this tunnel. Had they flooded the tunnel to keep invaders out? Or was it just simply muddy? What does it matter? We're in it now.

'Look, gentlemen, our intelligence tells us that this is a fair-sized complex. Of course, we want you to spread terror and fear wherever you go. And, whenever possible, to bring back as much information as you can. You are dismissed!'"

"I have to admit, that 'terror and fear wherever you go' struck an odd chord on my brain. I don't know why but that 'terror and fear' stuck in my head. I had never thought of myself as a 'terrorist'. I was simply a man doing what he had been trained to do. 'Mr. Strings' felt the same way."

"Melvin, ol' stick, don't get bent out of shape about a label. You're always going to be who you are, no matter wot? Right?"

I had to agree with him. But there was a bunch of stuff beginning to whirl around in my mind, like what is all of this about? Well, anyway I had to put all of that thought filled stuff on hold down there in this, tunnel.

They had told us that this was a fair-sized complex, whatever that meant. Believe me, Willie, ol' stick, slogging thru a muddy tunnel on your elbows and knees can really mess with your mind."

"Rufus, I'm feeling you, my brother, I'm feeling you."

The traffic had done this accordion back up thing on us again. O well…

"Turning a corner in the tunnel, we saw a bright light. A bright light at the end of the tunnel?"

Listening to Rufus and at the same time, paying close attention to this SUV that seemed to be determined to slash across my right side, while we're slogging down the freeway in a semi-lock down mode. I gave the errant driver 'the Finger' and kept my attention focused on Rufus's narrative.

"We crawled a little more carefully … and then turned the corner where the light was coming from, an unnaturally bright light for a tunnel. 'Mr. Strings' gave me the Now! Signal and we stood up and charged into this brightly lit room, bullets plunking out of our pistols at each person in the room.

It was not 'wild cowboy' shooting. We shot quickly, but precisely. 'Mr. Strings' plunked two uniformed women standing next to an operating table. And then popped two shots into the figure laying on the table. I plunked two rounds into the person who turned from the table to face me. Five shots and it was all over.

We stood for a minute, looking over the scene. It was a hospital operating room. The two people that 'Mr. Strings' had shot were nurses. And the people laying on the operating table was a pregnant woman, about to give birth. The person I shot was the doctor. No time for reflection, no time to waste.

We slithered back to where we had come in. I couldn't help thinking – I shot a doctor. I killed a doctor. It was like I had killed a priest."

I got lucky and made it back to Long Beach before 9 pm.

"You a good driver, Willie. If you hadn't ran over the speed limit when we broke free of the traffic, we'd still be stuck."

I didn't ask for Rufus's permission, I just drove him 'round behind the liquor store. Mr. Kim waved at us as he went into the back entrance. Rufus waved back and cracked out of the side of his mouth."

I'm glad Joe Kim is already married." That was all he said as he shuffled out of the car.

"Oh, Rufus, same time tomorrow?"

He did his little hip dip back to the car.

"I don't think tomorrow would be good for me, Willie. I feel like I need to do a rest time, you know what I mean? It's like every time I talk about that thing with the doctor, down in the tunnel, I feel a little bit zapped out afterwards."

"I understand. Well, I'll check with you day after tomorrow. O.k.?"

"Yeah, that'll be cool."

I remained in place, watching him make his hip-dip-strut to this nice little tent he had. "Tarzan," his feral cat-friend, pranced out of the shadows to greet him. Two of a kind. Now, home to talk to my lady.

I was preparing to leave a long love lorn message after four rings. ZiZi picked up on the fifth ring.

"O Willie, I was taking a hot, stress relieving bath. I'm so glad you called."

I felt like my heart was thumping a hole in my chest to hear her voice. After listening to Rufus all afternoon, ZiZi's voice was a beautiful sound.

"I've been with Rufus most of the afternoon and I just wanted to hear your voice before I started doing my homework for the night. And what are you stressed about?"

I felt that I could imagine her taking a deep breath.

"Maybe stressed is the wrong word. Maybe I should say pissed."

"About what?"

"About this 'I GAR Mfing-M' who's running around the country lying, spreading poison everywhere, causing people to get sick, and have a lot of them die."

"A Mexican brother calls him El Tramposo."

Her soft laughter was like bells ringing in my ears.

"One of the guys in our office came up with 'I GAR Mfing-M.' He says these letters stand for 'Ignorant Greedy Ass Racist M-fing Moron.' It's kind of long, but you know how lawyers are …' ."

I loved talking to ZiZi. She could go out there, but come back down to Earth in a sentence.

"But there's no need to talk about the president beast dog, let's talk about us."

And that's what we did for the next hour and fifteen minutes. The conversation went to a lot of corners.

"Willie, you say Rufus is living in a tent, he's homeless?"

"Yeah, I've seen his tent."

"I'm not going to suggest that you become his guardian or anything like that, but wouldn't it be easier for you to interview him at your place? That is, 'til I arrive."

"I'll give that some thought. You did say you were coming after the election. Right?"

"I hate to tell you, but they've asked me, begged me to stay until mid-December. We're dealing with a really important case. I laid the foundation for it and they've asked me to see it thru."

"Well, what if they want to have you go into January or February?" I know I sounded snarky.

"Don't be angry. I've already told them that I'm booked to join the Cochrand Firm in January. But if you want me to put all of this down and join you after the election, I'll do it."

Truth be told I was halfway tempted to say – yeahhh! Cut it loose and come on down here, I need you more than they do. But I also felt that a compromise was the best way for us to begin a lifetime relationship.

"ZiZi, look, you're coming to spend the rest of your life, being married and all that, right?"

"Yes, Willie, that's right."

I just loved to hear her jaws snapped shut on "that's right".

"So, why would I want to be so selfish as to ask you to give up something important, just because I'm greedy for your presence?"

"Willie, you are such a lousy diplomat. I can see, what you're doing, you're making me feel indebted to you. And I am, because a lot of men wouldn't do what you're doing."

"Well, what can I say? I'm just doing what I think will be in our mutual interest."

There was a long pause. Was she crying? What?

"Willie, look, look, this is September. We have almost three more months to be held apart by circumstances beyond our control. Just let me say that, if you think you'll need to see me before December, just say the word and I'll jump on the sky-bus, mask in place, and I'll be in your arms before the weekend."

"And bring some of that wonderful love with you when you come ..."

"Oh my God! You so nasty!"

"Talk to you tomorrow, baby."

"Talk to you tomorrow, too. And yeahhh, I'll bring all the wonderful love you'll ever need."

"ZiZi, I thought I was nasty."

"It takes one to know one."

Believe me, we were on the verge of making crossover flights; me to 'Frisco and her to LAX, before we ended our salacious telephonics. Yeahhh, ZiZi was the One. Time to get to the Rufus Outline.

Why do they call it "parsing?" Or something like that? That's what I was doing when I worked Rufus's story into prose that would reflect his voice, his vibe, his Him. The guy's stuff was so rich, filled with so many twists and turns.

The streets of Chicago, the Australian thing. The jungles of Viet Nam and underneath. The politics of the time. Could I separate that from the racism of the time? The notes, the outline that I had gave me a lot to do, but I didn't feel overwhelmed. I had a great character and a very creative world to explore. It was 2 am before my ass began to drag. Time to put things on hold 'til the next day.

I spent the whole day writing the stuff I needed to write about what I was going to write for Melvin Montaigne Dixon, III a.k.a. "Likka Sto' Rufus". I felt compelled to get it right to say it right. I was actually writing at different times and went back to the beginning, just to make sure that I had the right flavor, that I hadn't "juiced" it up just to satisfy my own ego. He wasn't into that -- "Ya know wot ahmsayin?" "It be like." "Like, you know?" "Like, it be like...", etc., etc., etc.

As a matter of fact, upon reflection, I came to the conclusion that he spoke grammatically clear English.

I found myself wondering – how did that happen? Being from Chitown myself, I was fully cognizable of the fact that there was a whole collection of brothers who might've been so deeply into the "patois," so linguistically entrenched, that it might've been necessary to speak the "patois" in order to legitimate yourself. But obviously, it wasn't that way with Rufus.

I was anxious to ask him about that, about a bunch of other questions. Like I said, I spent the whole day writing the stuff. I needed to write about what I was going to write for Melvin Montaigne Dixon, III a.k.a. "Likka Sto' Rufus".

CHAPTER 11

I tried to calm my heart rate down when I saw him standing, parade rest, in front of Mr. Kim's store. I hadn't prepared a Plan B, for, if he wasn't there. It was ten minutes to 2.

He acknowledged my presence with a cool wave and hand language that said ... a few more minutes.

I sat there, staring at this little strong man, a pan handler, a person of principle, who refused to accept coins. I was tempted to laugh out loud, really loudly, as I watched him return some coins (obviously coins) to a very conservatively dressed, middle aged, White male alcoholic. The dialogue was pure Rufus.

"Let me get something straight, sir. You've just purchased a fifth of good whisky, worth X number of dollars, just for you to go home, or wherever you're going to go. And you're going to walk past me and drop two lousy quarters in my hand. I find that highly unacceptable."

The would-be contributor was glazed in his tracks. Did I hear what I just heard? Did this pan handler, this beggar, question my contribution?

"I beg your pardon, sir, did you say what I just heard you say?"

Rufus was ruthless on this middle aged, White, male, alcoholic.

"That's right. You heard what I said. I don't have to repeat myself."

The White guy alcoholic dug down into his fashionable jeans.

"What if I gave you ten dollars?"

"Well, give it to me and stop posturing big White liberal man. And, no matter what you give me, it's not going to make you any less alcoholic. You gotta go somewhere and get some treatment for that. It's called alcoholism."

I watched the middle-aged White man stare at Rufus and then a sound erupted from his mask (the white one) that sounded like a scream.

I couldn't process what that was about. But I saw the White man throw the brown bag, filled with his favorite whisky, a few yards away from his expensive car, down on the ground.

He just threw it down on the ground in the mall parking lot, next to his car, jumped in and slowly clutched away. Rufus shuffled over to me a few minutes later.

"Hey, Willie, I got an appetite, why don't we go over to the Pho American, right here at Pacific and Pacific Coast Highway."

"I'm with you, my brother, I'm with you."

"I'm paying for this, so order what you want."

He was treating me to a meal at "The Pho American", a Vietnamese restaurant on Pacific Avenue and Pacific Coast Highway. I had passed the place many times, but had never thought to eat there.

"I don't know much about Vietnamese food."

"Well, take my word for it, you can't go wrong if you take Henry's suggestions. Yo Henry! Bring it over here and help my friend decide what he should eat."

Henry Le was the co-owner (with his sister) and had the attitude/ humor of a mischievous eight-year-old.

"Ah, welcome, my name is Henry, and I would suggest, since this is your first visit to an authentic Vietnamese restaurant, that you start your dinner off with our delicious gnat's nuts soup. And, for your entrée, we have the fried frog noses smothered in soy sauce. There will also be side dishes of tip toe cows tongue, sautéed bees' wings and marinated bok choi shoots."

If they had been able to contain themselves, just a little bit, they would've had me. But they couldn't contain their laughter, even behind their masks.

[Did I mention that we were being served in the spacious parking lot of "The Pho?" And they had done the Salamat Po thing of dividing the tables with plastic curtains, in a cubicle, plus placing the seats of the diners at a distance from each other. Their whole approach/protocol to the virus made me feel very safe.]

"Uhh, thank you very much for your suggestions, Mr. Le. Could I see a menu, please?"

They were almost rolling on the floor, laughing.

"We almost had you there for a minute, didn't we?"

I was forced to admit to Henry Le, the co-owner, that he had almost pulled my leg completely off. Rufus had gleeful tears in the corners of his eyes. And then it got serious. Henry had other customers to attend to.

"If you're a vegan, our brown noodle with vegetables is a good choice. And if you're a meat person, the beef pho is waiting for you. Enjoy your meal and welcome to the Pho American. Your waitress will be with you in a moment."

They had me hooked the moment they played their little routine on me. I've always loved to eat in restaurants where people showed that they had some sense of humor. We ordered bowls of beef pho.

Beef Pho at Henry's Place

"Rufus, how did you discover this place?"

He went into his thoughtful mode for a minute.

"I think it was the smell that drew me in. This was, like, last summer. I was just drifting around town, trying to figure out how I was going to get a few bucks, make it from one day to the next. And this Saigon smell hit my nose."

"What's a Saigon smell?"

"Well, they call it Ho Chi Minh City now, but I'm sure the smell is the same – garlicky, basil, fish sauce/nam phuck. I drifted to the entrance and took my position. I could see a lot of Mexicans going in and out. I knew I could make some money here because Mexicans are very generous people."

"Why do you think that is?"

"Hmmm, I never gave it a lot of thought. But, hey, just look around, Mexicans are hustlers, look at these people selling flowers on the corner, the dudes who make these fruit cups and stuff. I think that makes them a bit more sympathetic than lots of other people."

"That makes sense"

"Of course it makes sense, that's why I said it. Anyway, on my third day of standing a few feet from his front door, Henry came out to talk to me."

'Look, dude,' he said to me, 'if you're hungry I'll give you some food, but having you stand in front of our place makes us look bad, you know what I'm saying?'

"That was all he said, but he said it in the right way. Plus he gave me a carry out of fried fish and rice. And he stuffed a five-dollar bill into my breast pocket. I made a promise to myself that I would come over here whenever I could.

Ohh, here we go, here's our pho."

Two bowls as large as woks, filled to the brim with steaming beef broth, thin slices of beef, stuff on the side to toss into the mix: basil, bean sprouts, lime slices. It was hot and delicious. Not pepper hot, hot broth hot. I did a double take of Rufus using his chop sticks, well, of course, he had been to Viet Nam.

Viet Nam. Time to get back on the track.

"Rufus, during the course of our last meeting you mentioned something about your tunnel rat partner, 'Mr. Strings', and that he had, quote 'got his ass blown off.' Wanna talk about that? What happened?"

I think he was about to go into his spacey-thinking mode when this woman marched up to our table. It was a woman [I think] with a Marine drill sergeant's crew cut and a fire hydrant figure. She stood off to the side, observing plague protocol.

"Hey, Rufus, Henry tell me you are here – I come!"

"What's up, Miss Lady? How you doing?"

"Fine! Fine! Fine! Everything fine."

"That's good. Now you be good now – o.k.?"

"O.k., bye, bye." She waved her fingers at us and marched back into the restaurant.

"This is the person making all this good food. I can't remember her name. So I just call her Miss Lady."

We were half finished with our pho. I felt that I was about to pop open. Back to the track.

"Uhh, you were starting to tell me about 'Mr. Strings'."

He shook his head with fake exasperation.

"Willie, Willie, Willie, you are absolutely relentless, you know that?"

"I been called worse."

"I had been in 'Nam ten months and had disarmed more booby traps and crawled in and out of more tunnels than you could shake a stick at. In addition to everything else, a letter had finally reached me from Yvonne, to tell me that I had a two-month-old son."

"I have named him Melvin, Melvin. And I must tell you he looks like you."

"A man-child. Up 'til that time I hadn't given a lot of thought about being a Daddy. Or anything like that. I just went down into the tunnels and did my work. But now, I had a wild urge to get back to Australia to see my wife and baby boy. I put in for a thirty-day leave and got turned down."

"Why did they turn you down?"

"If you would stop trying to talk over me, I'll tell you. You want some dessert? Miss Lady makes a really good custard, but I have to warn you – it's got something in it that almost chases you to the potty."

"Ahhh, I think I'll have a cup of tea."

"Henry, you got time to give us two cups of tea?"

"I'll make time …"

"The excuse they gave me for not approving of my leave was that I hadn't been 'in country' long enough. Understand now, this is coming from the American side. I was in a nut grinder; I was an American attached to an Australian unit. And the American side didn't want to understand why an American should be given leave to go to Australia to be with his Australian Aborigine wife."

"A little taste of racism here, huh?"

"More than a little taste, but as luck would have it, Colonel (promoted) Knights Bridge was making an inspection tour and I managed to get an appointment with him. I got all spiffed up and knocked on the Colonel's door."

'Come in Private Dixon, have a seat and tell me what the bloody hell is going on?'

"I was five minutes into my story when his face started getting red. It was scary to see this man get mad. It was like he started boiling from the top all the way down to his shoe tops. Six minutes into my story, he was on the phone to Captain Beverhead."

"Rufus, are you kidding me? The man's name was really 'Beverhead'?"

"Swear on Granddaddy's grave. And when Colonel Knights Bridge got thru with him, you could've called him Cleaverhead."

Rufus took a sip of his tea, stroked his mustache left and right and sat up straight as a British Colonel. His British accent was pitch perfect.

"'Captain Beverhead, this is Colonel Malcolm Knights Bridge of the Australian Army's School of Military Engineering. We have one of your chaps attached to our unit. This man has been performing his duties in an exemplary manner. In many instances he has gone beyond the call of duty. Are you listening to me, Captain Beaver-Head?

This man had had his application for thirty-day leave to visit his wife and new born son rejected.

I want you to rescind that rejection. I want you to get on the stick immediately. Are you listening to me, Captain Beaver-Head? Good, that's exactly what I wanted to hear. You needn't worry about transport to Australia, we will take care of that. I would like to suggest that Private Dixon's leave application be approved and in his possession by the end of this working week. He <u>will</u> be able to board a military plane for Australia next Monday.

If this matter is not handled expeditiously, I shall be forced to take this matter to General Armstead and I can assure you that your Captain's bars will disappear so fast it will make your head swim. Have you heard me loud and clear, Captain Beaver-Head? Very good.'"

"So, that was taken care of. I stood and gave him the best British Army salute I could give. Colonel Knights Bridge returned my salute with a sly twinkle in his eyes."

'Carry on, Private Dixon, have a jolly good time in Sydney.'"

"Yessah!"

It seemed like time started dragging her heels the minute my leave paper was put in my hand. Captain Beaverhead delivered the paper himself.

"'Uhhh, sorry for the delay, Private, we had a little SNAFU ...'"

"Yessir, no problem sir."

"No need to push the Captain's face in it; I had my authorization to go to see my wife and son. I had three days 'til giddy up time. I didn't know what to do with myself. I didn't have to worry too much about what to do with myself. I didn't have to worry too much about what to do -- the Army can always find something for you to do. I could see it coming when 'Mr. Strings' shuffled up the center aisle of our barracks, a cigarette hanging out of the corner of his mouth."

"'Sorry to interrupt your beauty sleep, mite, but they've discovered a tunnel they want us to check out.'"

"No rest for the weary, huh?"

"You got that right, Willie man, you got that right."

"I had no idea where Viet Nam was on the planet. I guess it was located somewhere right underneath the sun because it was always hot and humid. Always. I can remember times when I actually wished that I was back in Chicago, in the snow."

Rufus was in his groove now. Sometimes, I noticed, it might take him a little while to get started, but once he found his groove, it was like listening to a movie. That's the way he spoke, like a movie.

"Blazing hot, so humid sweat would just run down your body like you were in a shower. The sweat ran down into my boots. I couldn't drink enough water.

'Awright man, listen up! If you wind up with an empty canteen, you're gonna be shit outta luck because there's no drinkable water in the immediate vicinity.'

Sergeant Roughnuts looked out for us; I have to give him that. And he seemed to have picked me out for special care because I was the only Black Yank in this Australian squad."

"'How you doin' mite?'

'I'll live, where is this tunnel we're 'sposed to be checking out?'

'Intel places it about a mile east of here.'

We had started out at dawn, and it was hot then. And we had another mile to hike thru this crazy ass jungle. We had already killed a dozen snakes and somebody on our left flank said they had spotted a tiger stalking us.

By the time we made it to the entrance of this tunnel, I was more than ready to go underground, it would be cool down there. Me and 'Mr. Strings' armed ourselves with our favorite weapons – the silencer on the pistol, a razor-sharp bayonet, a small flashlight.

The UNDERWORLD. Maybe I was becoming a rat. I could almost see in the dark. Interesting tunnel, it was low but wide enough for the two of us to crawl along, side by side. We had crawled about fifty yards when we came to this side room. Two men in dirty, mud crusted clothes were sleeping like dead men on a futon.

'Laborers', 'Mr. Strings' whispered to me. These poor people dudes were conscripts, people the Viet Cong used to dig these tunnels. We decided not to kill them, they would be a great source of info.

'Mr. Strings' took the one on the left, I took the one on the right. We woke them up with pistol barrels stuck in their ears. It doesn't take a lot of explanation when you have a pistol stuck in your ear. We made the universal gesture – finger on the lips – to be silent. And pushed them thru the tunnel we had just crawled thru.

Our people pulled them up and out. We had scored. These were people who had probably worked in other tunnels. And they probably had some valuable info about a number of things. They weren't soldiers, just people caught up in a nasty ass war. We had scored. Time to hike back to the Concern.

We shared some of our water with the captives. Poor guys were scared to death, they thought we were going to shoot them.

'Mr. Strings' eased up next to me before we started our hike back.

'Melvin, you got any shit sheets on yer? I gotta take a dump.' 'Mr. Strings' was very fastidious about some things. He never liked to use tree leaves or anything like that to wipe himself. I had a half roll of shit sheets in my backpack.

'They're kind of damp.'

'No problem, mite, no problem at all.'

He took the half roll of damp toilet paper and walked a few yards away, behind a big palm tree. I had taken a few steps when I heard this heavy whomp! sound. I stood in place, staring down at the ground for a full minute. I knew what whomp! meant. Only two things, either someone was firing a mortar at us, or somebody had stepped on a mine.

Our squad made a very careful rush to 'Mr. Strings' behind the big palm tree. We had to be careful, they were sure to have other booby traps planted around. 'Mr. Strings' was sprawled on his stomach, his pants down around his knees, his ass shredded to ribbons."

He paused to take a long, deliberate sip of his tea. I could see the scene so vividly in my mind's eye I felt like puking. Rufus gently placed his cup back on the table. He was a warrior, a strong man who knew how to keep a grip on himself. That's what he was demonstrating to me.

"He had stepped on one of these little mines that the Cong had designed to go off by sense detection. These Viet Cong had perfected some incredible shit to fight us with.

'Mr. Strings' was messed up, suffering like a big dog. Sergeant Roughnuts was on the phone, calling for a helicopter to come for the wounded man. 'Mr. Strings' seemed to be in another place. He was calm. I went up close to him and knelt down.

'Shoot me, mite.'

He said it loud enough for the people near me to hear him. They all turned to look at me.

'I can't do it 'Strings', I can't shoot you, man.'

Sergeant Roughnuts came to kneel beside me.

'We can't shoot you, d'yer understand? We can't shoot you.' But then, the sergeant reached underneath 'Mr. Strings's body, pulled his tunnel rat pistol from his shoulder holster and placed it near 'Mr. Strings's right hand.

It seemed like all of the jungle chatter that you would normally hear, bird noises, monkeys screeching and screaming, insects, all of it suddenly stopped. Jungle flies were clustering on 'Mr. Strings' s ripped up backside like bees to honey. We just stared at the scene in front of us, barely breathing.

'Mr. Strings's right hand was moving very slowly toward the pistol. The minute he gripped the handle it was like someone who had a familiar tool in his hand; a hammer, a fork, a spoon, something he was totally at ease with.

He pulled the pistol on the ground, right to his forehead, winked at me and blew his brains out. There was no sobbing and weeping, no sanctimonious bullshit. I think we felt good about what had happened. 'Mr. Strings' had taken himself out of a life that was going to be filled with operations and pain."

That was it. Nothing else to say on this particular day.

"Hey Henry, we're getting ready to split, you wanna collect this money or not?"

I stood off to one side, staring at Rufus and the Vietnamese man, Henry Le. Henry looked to be about half Rufus's age. He must've been in Viet Nam before America was trying to Agent Orange the country to death. I had to ask Rufus the inevitable question.

"Rufus, Henry knows you're a Viet Nam vet, right?"

"O yeahh, that came out a couple days after he shooed me away from the front of his restaurant."

"So, what's the vibe? How do you all square things?"

"Well, first thing you gotta remember – the war was over when Henry came along. What is he? About forty or so. He came along when they had American Army stuff in museums in Saigon, uhh Ho Chi Minh City. They talk about it like it's ancient history or something. They call it 'The American War', but they don't blame Americans for the war, they blame the American government. Makes sense, huh?"

"Yeah, I guess you could say that."

This interview/story day was over. I drove around behind Mr. Kim's liquor store to Rufus's tent. Tarzan was waiting, cat like, next to the tent. I couldn't resist asking – "Rufus, you o.k, man?"

"Naw, I ain't o.k. Look around you, Willie, is anybody o.k.?"

What kind of reply could I make to that?

"Tomorrow?"

"If I don't get my ass blown off tonight."

I sat in my car, watching him disappear in his tent, not knowing whether to laugh or cry.

CHAPTER 12

"Sydney, Australia. Lord Almighty! It was like being airlifted from Hell to Heaven. Well, it wasn't quite Heaven-Heaven, but it was a long, long way -- way from the Hell of Vietnam.

Yvonne met me with baby Melvin in her arms and I stepped onto a love roller coaster for the next thirty days. Check it out, Willie lad ... I was a twenty-three-four – however, I was, Daddy. Married to a forty-thousand-year-old woman."

We were back at the Salamat Po, our resident hang out.

"Rufus, just talk to me about what it was like, what it felt like for you to be in Australia, with a wife and child..."

"What did you think I was going to talk about? This weird experience that I had in Saigon, with this Tai Chi master who had just escaped from the Viet Cong? This woman who had learned how to forecast the future ..."

"What did she tell you?"

"I'm not going to tell you."

We were back in what had become our favorite restaurant, the Salamat Po, and Rufus was fencing off my questions like a master fencer.

"So, why don't you just tell me what you want to tell me?"

"That's just what I was getting ready to do, before you started pecking at me."

"Sorry."

"Ain't no real big thang. Yvonne and the baby, that took a minute to get used to. When I left, she wasn't pregnant. Well, not right then anyway, but soon after. And I'm back on the scene many months later and I got a two-month old son.

In addition to a whole bunch of other things. I was prepared to have our taxi take us back to this shanty town where she lived. No good.

'Where is this?' I asked her when she directed the taxi driver into these really nice homes. They called them 'Council Apartments'.

'I didn't want to raise our child in the shanty town'.

I didn't have to argue with her about that. But how did she do it. How did she rise from the shanty town to this?"

'Melvin, I have to tell you, your commanding officer, Major Knights Bridge ...'

'He's a Colonel now.'

'Well, blessings on him. He had a member of his staff come and chat with me after you were deployed to Viet Nam. This lady.'

'A woman?'

'Yes, Captain Powers. She took down a lot of info, asked me what I needed and all that. It was clear that your allotment would be welcome, but beyond that? I made it plain that I would need a proper environment to raise my child in. I didn't bite my tongue. I told her straight up – I don't see why I, the wife of an American soldier, should be forced to raise a child in the slums of Sydney.

As you can see, they did something about my situation.'

"Willie, can you dig the scene? This young wife was pulling strings had pulled strings to improve her station in life for her child's sake. I was bowled over. Coupled to that, she was going to school four days a week, carrying the baby in a basket."

'Mom is going to start keeping him when I get into my sophomore year.'

"To do what?"

"She was studying to be a social psychologist. Can you get ready for that, Willie man?"

Rufus's voice was approaching the loud level again. I gestured for him to be cool.

"Sorry 'bout that. But, hey, look at this ... I left this girl-woman and I came back a year later and she has my son, and has created a whole new life for herself. She was studying to become a social psychologist."

"Why social psychologist?"

"The way she explained it to me was that her people needed some people to help them, to create an understanding of where they were, what they were going thru, how they could move on …."

"Rufus, I don't know a lot about social psychology, but I've never heard of a social psychologist who makes it better for their people by getting a degree."

"Well, that goes to prove a point. Social psychologists improve people's lives by explaining what they have done, what they are doing, and what they could be doing."

"Oh," I felt like I had been chastised. Rufus hit me with one of his sneaky-snarky eye rolls.

"Don't feel bad. Yvonne did me just like I did you. We're never too old to learn something, or something new. Right?"

I agreed with him by slapping a low high five across the table.

CHAPTER 13

"I was a loonng way from being ready to go back to the war zone when my leave time came. Me and Yvonne had <u>really</u> gotten to know each other. You know what I'm saying? Early on, to be honest, there was this deep physical attraction thing."

"I know a little bit about that."

"Well then, you know what I'm talking about. We had that going too, for sure, but then we really got deep into stuff. I called her my 'forty-thousand-year-old wife' because she could get into that Dream-Time stuff. And a whole bunch of other stuff that I didn't know squat about.

I was the slum bred brother from Chicago and she was the daughter of the Original people. That was the way she put it.

'The White people named us Aboriginals. We have always called ourselves 'The Original People'.' We got so close, so deep into each other during my leave; we could actually have differences of opinions about different things. She thought that it was wrong for America and Australia to be in Southeast Asia altogether, in Viet Nam."

"It's simply another Anglo colonial power play. Look, the French were there and discovered that they couldn't beat the Vietnamese to their knees. So, the Americans decided to take over where the French left off."

"This was to stop the spread of Communism from taking over the whole place, right?"

'Melvin, read my lips', she suggested, 'What sense does it make to say that you're trying to stop the spread of Communism from North Viet Nam to South Viet Nam when Big Bad China is strongly behind the North. Sorry, my husband, but you're destined to lose this one.'

We had to let it go at that point. But I have to admit – she really started me to thinking. She had planted some ideas, some thoughts that I had never considered before. Make a long story short, I started thinking about <u>not</u> going back to Nam at the end of my leave. Yvonne counseled me; 'No, please don't do that, Melvin. They'll put you in jail for years, for deserting.'"

"Desertion, during time of war is considered treason, and you could be executed."

"Willie! You too cold! Shut up! You sound like Yvonne!"

Rufus could mimic the late Little Richard's sarcastic audience-friendly, sassy put down to a T.

"I got on the plane back to Hell, to crawl back into the tunnels. That was just about the way it went. The plane landed on Monday at midnight and I was back down in the tunnels on Wednesday."

"Sorry to interrupt your beauty sleep, ol' stick, but it looks like your expertise is needed…."

"I was back down in the tunnels again. But I didn't like it this time around. Kind of hard to explain.

Early on, working with my partner, 'Mr. Strings,' it was sort of an adventure. I was scared shitless most of the time, but there was still a sense of adventure about the whole thing. It didn't help matters a whole lot when they partnered me up with this wild kid from a sheep ranch. Aussies speak this brand of English they call "Strine." Strine, rhymes with drain. This kid spoke a 'strine' that was so thick I could barely understand a word he said. I was the twenty-three-year old 'Elder', he was my apprentice.

He lasted exactly three days. It didn't happen in the tunnel, it happened out on patrol. He picked up a booby trapped plastic doll and it blew his head half way off."

I felt I had heard enough for one day, I wanted to stop hearing about all of this ugly shit, this madness.

Rufus had a hard expression on his face, but he asked, in a very gentle voice; "You want me to stop talking about this crazy-mad shit?"

"No, don't stop, I need to hear this because it's what I'm writing about."

We ordered more tea and he kept talking ….

"After the kid was blown away I don't think I had another sober day, for years afterward.

Thing you have to remember about Nam, man, it's that the whole scene was so, so sur ... so...."

"Surrealistic?"

"That's when things are too real to be true, right?"

"Best definition I can think of."

"So, that's what it was – surr-realistic. A lot of us got high on something and stayed high most of the time. Everybody smoked weed, that was like nothing. Some of us fell into a heron bag.

Some of us mixed pills and beer together. Every day was surr-realistic. It was 'specially surr-realistic out in the boonies, in the field. Check this out. It had gotten to the point, in my mind, that I felt like I should defect to the Viet Cong."

"Why would you do that? Wouldn't they kill you?"

"Answer to question number one. I would defect because I could see that we were losing the war. An idiot could see that. If I defected I would be on the winning side. See how warped my thinking was at that time?"

Would they kill me? Maybe, maybe not. I had got hold of a lot of propaganda pamphlets and stuff, about the fact that we were over there fighting and dying for the White people.

This is the kind of stuff I had going on in my mind as I drug my body thru this tunnel; tunnel nine- thousand and forty-two, something like that. Or seemed to be. Yeah, I had made up my mind. If I ran into any Congs down in this tunnel I was going to surrender to them, defect.

But that wasn't what happened. I crawled to one of these rooms where they used as meeting places. Nobody on the scene. They may have been there ten minutes before I got there, or an hour before. But there was nobody there when I got there.

I was relieved, to say the least. I had already changed my mind about defecting, half way in my crawl thru the tunnel. And I was grateful that I didn't have to kill anybody. And there was nobody on the scene to kill me.

I started my crawl back to the tunnel opening. Damn. I felt something like a hundred needles stick into both of my knees at the same time as I crawled thru a section of the tunnel. Damn, what the hell is this?

I was on the verge of screaming like a crazy baby when they pulled me up from the tunnel. I couldn't figure out what was happening. They rushed me to the medic, everybody call him 'Doc.'

'Doc, what's going on here?! I feel like I have needles burning in my knees!'

'From what I can see, you're about right. You do have needles in your knees.' I don't know why, but that struck a funny chord in my head. Needles in my knees. Get it, Willie? Needles in my knees."

What else could I do but nod? Yeah, I get it. Needles in your knees. There was nothing about that that sounded funny to me.

❧

"I have to give it to 'em, stuff had started moving faster in 'Nam than it had ever moved. It took them about two hours to 'copter me out of the boonies to the base hospital. The problem was that it took them a little longer to detail what had happened to me.

I thought it was kinda interesting what this young doctor, Dr. Choi was his name, explained – 'O.k., so here's the story, soldier. You crawled into the tunnel. No problem – right? Now, when you turn around to crawl out, the Viet Cong had calibrated a booby trap arrangement with hundreds of toothpick sized punji sticks. You're familiar with punji sticks. Right? Right.

So, as you're crawling out, these sticks slant up. You know? Like how your car can get trapped on one of those traps that will permit you to roll forward, but will spike your tires if you back up. That's what happened with you.

The toothpick punji sticks that feel like needles to you have been 'marinated' in some kind of nerve deadening substance, let's call it a poison. We don't have all of the diagnostic and therapeutic facilities to treat your problem, so we're shipping you off to our hospital in Mannheim, Germany. Good luck, soldier.'

So, there I was, up shit's creek without a paddle. One thing I can say – they drugged me up pretty good for my trip to Germany."

I had this guilty feeling that we were taking hold of our Salamat Po table a bit too long, but when Rufus stepped to the men's to release some of his tea, Lola placed a fresh pot of tea on our table and winked. We were cool.

I think it was one of the first times in my life that I was grateful that I was in a restaurant that didn't serve beer. Tea was just right for me, for the moment.

"I came to my senses listening to a couple young studs explaining to me why they were going to have to cut off my legs, just a bit above the knees. 'You are not going to cut off my legs.'

That's what I said to them, and I meant it. I was prepared to bite somebody to death to stop these eager beavers from sawing my legs off.

I have to give it to these guys, they were really patient with me. They explained."

'Look, soldier, we've managed to extract all of these punji toothpicks out of your knees, but whatever they smeared on these sticks has damaged the nerves in your knees. We're not sure, but we think that you might be on the way to a bad case of gangrene. In other words, if the gangrene settles in, you'll have a serious problem.'

"I can't remember what I said to them, what kind of plea I copped. But they listened; they gave my legs a second chance. From that time on, like every two or three hours or so, I had somebody putting something into my body.

And as you can see, even with your thick glasses, I still have my legs and I'm here, loud and clear."

"I heard that …."

Maybe my statement sounded a bit sarcastic, judging from the warped smile he flashed across the table.

"Saved my legs and lost my soul. I guess that's one way to describe what happened."

"What happened?"

"I knew you were going to ask that. Why don't we get into that tomorrow, I got a terrible headache."

"Sorry, Rufus, you should've told me."

"What could you do? You got a cure for the kind of headaches I have?"

I decided not to even try to answer his question; I had learned how to go with the Rufus flow.

"Willie, I got your message. Sorry I wasn't here when you called, I had to work late. I hope all is going well with you. And your work. I miss you very much and I'm counting the days 'til we'll be together. That's all I have to say right now. Let's talk tomorrow – I'll be home by six.

Can you believe that any human being could lie as often and as badly as this beast monster so-called President can lie? Oh, well, I guess we should be used to it by now.

How's Rufus going? Talk to you tomorrow."

I re-played ZiZi's response to my earlier call, just to listen to her voice. *"How's Rufus going?"* That was her question. I sat at my kitchen table and forced myself to review my "Rufus file," to go thru the pile of notes I had accumulated, that I was accumulating --*"How's Rufus going?"*

I left the kitchen table and sprawled on the sofa in my front room. Click the remote. O God, not him again. What did ZiZi call him? – "this beast monster." No one could ever think of a more accurate name. How can "beast monster" stand behind this pulpit and tell so many blatant, outrageous lies. The country is being eaten alive by a plague and he's telling all of these lies, giving all of this mis-information out.

Enough of this madness. Wonder what Rufus meant when he asked me? "You got a cure for the kind of headaches I have?" I'll have to probe that a bit when we get back together.

I have to admit, I was on the cusp of panic after driving past the liquor store parking lot, driving back past the liquor store after an hour at the beach. Parking for another hour. Where was he? After three days, I almost panicked. Maybe he's dead. Maybe he's committed suicide? The veteran suicide rate was sky high.

"Oh, yes, he is asleep."

Mr. Kim was busy selling booze, so he didn't have time to explain why his backyard tenant was asleep. I went back to my car, to think things out for a bit. It was twelve o'clock, high noon. His pan handling hours, like clockwork, were from eleven to two.

I went back to the car, sat there thinking on the situation real hard for a half an hour. What the hell! I decided to grab the cat by the tail. I drove around thru the alley behind Mr. Kim's store and parked as close to the side of the alley as I could. I had to see what was happening with the brother.

"Rufus, it's me, Willie...."

"What're you doing out there, c'mon in."

What's that old cliché? I was pleasantly surprised at what I found inside his tent. He was laying on a thick futon against the wall, right over there, and there was a chair, one of those low slung garden deals at the opposite wall. That was the "furniture". Aside from the neat stacks of books surrounding the sides of the tent.

"You have to keep your mask on in here 'cause there's not too much circulation." He pulled a mask from a hanger near him and strung it behind his ears. I had to crouch a bit, but that was the only discomfort. He let me do the surreptitious study thing for a few beats.

"Sit down, have a seat. What's happening?"

I felt tempted to start off at a high tempo, a fever-breathless question – where you been, man?! But I knew better. I settled into the lawn chair, very comfortable, a place to rest your legs in front of you.

"Hadn't seen you for a few days, just wondering where you were, what was happening with you?"

He plopped himself up on a fat round pillow and stared at me for a few intense seconds.

"I've been walking."

"Walking?" I could always hear myself sounding slightly idiotic whenever I repeated what he said to me.

"Yeahhh, I had a lot on my mind after we met last time."

"Like what? And what did walking have to do with it?"

I could almost see thru his mask, at the sarcastic curl of his mouth.

"Willie West, I got to give it to you, man, you are a persistent cookie, you know that?"

"I've been called worse." I'm sure he could imagine my grim smile behind my mask.

"Well, just let me say this; I've done a lot of walking, a lot of thinking as I walked, over the years..."

I watched him settle back on his pillow, to lace his hands behind his head. I went on Rufus alert. I had to be careful to not allow him to begin to "meander" on me. We were in full Rufus-Willie Mode Operation.

"You went walking for three days...'"

"Not days, only at night. I've been sleeping days."

"And you were thinking about what happened in your life after you got out of the hospital, after the knee surgeries and all that?"

He slumped and seemed to surrender, but I had to be careful, he could detour in a split sentence.

"Yeahhh, there was a lot of that on my mind."

"I remember you saying .... 'saved my legs and lost my soul'."

"Yeah, that's what I said. You got me, Willie, straight up."

"So, how did you lose your soul?"

I felt like biting my tongue, but it was too late.

"Well, since it seems like you really want to know, let me tell you. They dropped me off in Chicago after my hospital stay in Germany. I wanted to go to Australia, to be with my woman, who was, surprise! Surprise! Pregnant with our second child. It was a beautiful loving time we spent together during my thirty-day leave.

'No,' they said to my request to go to Australia.

We went round 'n round on that one. They dropped all kinds of arguments on me.

'Look, soldier, you enlisted in Chicago and that's your home of record, so that's where were going to discharge you.' That was the 'nasty cop'. Here's what the 'good cop' laid on me, gently, smoothly. A brother. 'Melvin, look man, they ain't got no V.A. facilities nowhere in Australia, so far as I know. Now then, from looking at your medical records 'n stuff, you're gonna be needing follow up treatment for years to come.

Now then, let's say you manage to get back to Australia, with no V.A. available to you, what's gonna happen to you, man? You know we got the best health care system in the world, right up in here. Why go somewhere else and gamble your life away?'

The 'bad cop' was really the one that pissed me off the most.

'Look, Private Dixon, we don't find it to be an urgent thing for you to get back to Australia, to be with this native woman whose 'sposed to be your wife. That's number one. Number two, the Army is not able to process the period of your injury with the time you were deployed to Viet Nam.'

'I was a tunnel rat, attached to the Australian Army of Engineering.'

'What the hell is a 'tunnel rat'?'

"They took you thru a lot, huh?"

"Yeah, they took me thru a lot, but I fought back."

Rufus braced himself up on his elbows; I watched his small body become a hard fist.

"I fought back, Willie! Yessir! I fought back! The dirty bastards wouldn't allow me to return to Australia 'because of budgetary considerations', but I was able to have this stingy ass pension, which I had to fight for—electronically deposited to Yvonne in Australia. At least, I could say to my wife and children (baby coming) that I cared about them."

CHAPTER 14

"Awright, I'm back in Chicago. Homeless. Jobless. ('No openings for an ex-tunnel rat, pal. Sorry.') And I had this fifty-thousand-pound monkey on my back."

"You were hooked, a junky, an addict?"

I don't know why it seemed to be the perfect afternoon to talk about "soul losing". The late afternoon sun streamed thru the red, green, yellow canvass that covered our heads. I felt that it was exactly the right stage for the scene.

"Yeahh, I was a dope fiend. No need to sugar coat things with words like 'addict'. A dope fiend is a fiend for dope. That's what I was. Back tracing, it came from all of the stuff that they gave us in the hospital. But I'm not going to lay all of the blame on them.

I have to take responsibility for deciding to get on heron...."

(Funny, I noticed, early on, that ol' time dope fiends never pronounced the name of the drug as it was written in the medical journals, "heroin". They always said "heron," like that skinny necked bird.)

"How long were you on heron?"

I had to decipher the muffled laugh beyond the mask.

"Willie, trust me, you ain't never 'off' heron. You can stop using for ten years, but that does not mean you are 'off'. Heron is a mighty monkey. The fact that I have not used for twenty years or so, does not mean I'm clean. The fact of the matter, as they like to say these days, is that I used for about twenty years, give or take a few months."

He was silent after that statement, as though he was waiting for my reaction. I didn't disappoint his expectations.

"You were a dope fiend for twenty years?"

114

I tried to make myself sound blasé, but I didn't pull it off. I sounded incredulous, even to myself.

"You were a dope fiend for twenty years?!"

Once again, there was this silent period, this cool delay.

"Yeahhh, I got lucky. Not a lot of ex-dope fiends around who managed to survive twenty years on the 'Horse'. That's what they used to call it; 'Horse'. I can lay up here and say – I rode the 'Horse' or maybe the 'Horse' rode me. The other thing that they used to say, if you had a habit, is that you had a monkey on your back."

"Sounds like a dope fiend was locked into a cage full of animals."

I can't say what it is that made me make a comment like that, but Rufus found it really funny. He pulled his mask down to laugh. Brother had a funny/freaky sense of humor. I jumped right back on the track, fearful of losing the thread.

"So, you were on the 'Horse' for twenty years? Anything happen that was interesting during the course of those years?"

I was learning, intuitively, I guess, how to drill/drain stuff out of Rufus. He laid on his futon, masked up. And I sprawled on a plastic covered lawn chair, opposite. A good social distance away from each other. It was like a shrink-patient set up, except for the fact that I wasn't a shrink and he wasn't a patient. I was a writer and he was the main character of a story that I was writing. I didn't have to remind myself that I was dealing with an unusual character; he reminded me.

"Willie, I know you're trying to play on me by asking me – '... Anything happen that was interesting during the course of those years?' O.K., that's fair, that's cool. Maybe I can think of a few things..."

Forty-five minutes later, after he had filtered from one crazy-mad-weird-incredible-believable/unbelievable story to another, I had to pull him to a halt.

"Rufus, I'm hungry."

"Me too."

That's what caused him to agree to come to the end of a weird story about having hooked up with a Russian oligarch cartel ("way back when") who had decided that they were going to hijack the mind of the next guy that they felt they would be able to totally control, "The President."

"So, how did you become involved in this?"

"I was 'out there', Willie man, I was '*out there*'. Ain't no telling who you're going to deal with, when you're '*out there*'. The thing you have to keep in mind is that I was a freako in the dope fiend/habitual criminal world.

I was somebody who had crawled thru North Vietnamese tunnels. I had shot people to death. I had done a whole bunch of negative stuff, but I wasn't a criminal-animal, like a lot of those people were. I <u>was</u> an animal, that's true, but I was a well-trained ex-tunnel rat, not a criminal. You dig where I'm coming from?"

We decided to have a snack at Salamat Po.

It always surprised me a little bit to receive this fo' real reception we got when we went to this place.

"Your table is ready." That was the way Lola welcomed us.

"I was praying to God Almighty that it would be," Rufus responded. Weird person, I could never tell what he was going to say. We took our table and de-masked. That was a pleasure. I was feeling deprived of some kind of stimuli by not being able to see people's faces.

"You were talking about being a dope fiend for twenty years?"

"I knew I could count on you to remind me. You mind if I have a sip of this tea before I spill out my dope guts to you?"

"Thanks, darling."

I swear, I could almost see our waitress blush behind her mask, "Thanks darling." He could turn it on and off whenever he wanted to.

"What you have to understand about that heron thing is that it can place you in a very special category. Let's have some of that chicken adobo and rice?"

"You got it."

Midafternoon, 1:30, a perfect time. Just after lunch and a couple hours before the evening eaters showed up.

"Heron, a special category?"

"Yes, that's what I think, my own personal opinion."

"How so?"

"Damn, man, why don't you slow down a bit? You make me feel like we're on Sixty Minutes or something."

I could see, from that snarky twinkle in his eyes that he was just messin' with me.

"Sorry, Mr. Rufus, suh, I didn't mean to anger you none." My best Southern drawl. He liked that so much he laughed out loud.

"That's cool, Willie, that's good. You sound almost authentic. Now then, where was I?"

"Heron, a special category?"

"Yeah, think about it. Charlie Parker, Bella Lugosi, Lady Day, Errol Flynn, Alexander the Great, Nero, Miles Davis, Juanita Jones, most of the dudes that I grew up with on the Southside of Chicago, hundreds; I could sit here and name names all day long. And the thing that put them in a special category, including me, is that we all had some kind of talent."

We had to pause for a few minutes to get into our chicken adobo, but I could tell he was energized, into his groove.

"When I was using heavy I felt like I was on another planet. It was like I could hear stuff that 'normal' people couldn't hear. I could become invisible, if my fix was right."

"Invisible?"

"You heard me, mister, I could become invisible. That's how I got away with so much devilment. I could walk into a place, let's say, like this place. Walk behind the counter, open the cash register, take the money and split."

"Without anybody seeing you?"

"Well, sometimes. It had a lot to do with the quality of the dope. This special thing I'm talking about was almost some kind of Blessing. Look at this; I never had a cold when I was using. That made me think that heron is probably a cure for the common cold."

A chicken bone from the adobo almost got stuck in my throat. "Huh?"

"Heron caused me to come to Heavenly California."

We both paused to suck on our adobo chicken thigh bones. Delicious food.

"I was hanging out in a shootin' gallery. Willie, you know what a shootin' gallery is?"

"It's a funky, filthy ass place where bona fide dope fiends go to shoot dope."

"Damn, brother man, that's the absolute dirty dog truth."

"Rufus, I get the impression that you forget that I'm from Chicago too."

He sounded very sincere and serious when he said; "I have to remind myself to remember that. Anyway, there I am in this funky, filthy ass place with my homies; 'Dukey Dog', 'Cornbread Charlie', we called him that because he was from some lil' ol' town in Miss'ssippi, Weird Jones Buttons, Bishop Jones, the usual bunch.

We were shooting this exceptionally good heron from Mexico, straight. Had been doing it for a whole day, watching the snow come down like big clouds. Terrible snow. I got into this dope fiend conversation with my boy 'Dukey'. Dope fiend conversation, punctuated by us nodding off on each other from time to time. I forget what the so called conversation was, but he mumbled 'California' about four or five times.

I asked him one serious question – 'Is it warm all the time?'

'Yeahhh, it's warm all the time, and they got heron like this in every bag.'

Two days later, I was on my way to California. It took me almost a year to get here, 'cause I got waylaid by a whole bunch of things, including a ninety-day stay in a funky little jail in New Mexico, or maybe it was Arizona. In any case, as you can see – I made it. It was my twenty-year journey into Southern, no, Northern California heron life. Gotta keep stuff straight. I landed in Northern California first and the drug scene was superb, but it got real chilly in the winter, so I decided to come down south; the first time I had decided to go South anywhere. You know what I mean?"

"I had left the snow, but now, for the first time in my life, I felt snowed in. Can you dig where I'm coming from, Willie man?"

I simply nodded yes, I didn't want to distract him with any words from me.

"I stole children's bicycles off of ghetto back porches to support my habit. I stole people's sheets off of their backyard clothes lines in deepest Watts. I performed homosexual acts…."

I signaled for more tea as he paused, this spaced away look in his eyes. Lola took two minutes to replace our empty tea pot.

"I raided church boxes. I think I could say I basically ravaged Southern California, busting windows out of parked cars to get at whatever was in the car. From all over El-A to San Diego and back. I would do anything for a fix. I paid a helluva price for what I did, believe me.

I was in and out of jail on a regular basis. In a way I almost welcomed the bust because the thirty-day-bit -- the ninety-day-bit would give me a chance to lower my intake need. The problem was that I would be a real hog when I got back on the streets. I might double my heron intake out of pure greed. I must've gone thru a dozen re-hab programs. Some judges would check out my war injuries and go easy on me. Others just got tired of looking at my sorry ass and gave me as much time as they could…."

"Rufus, I hate to interrupt, but I'm just curious about something …."

"I know, my relationship with Yvonne and my sons.

She had another boy. She named him Ervin; Melvin and Ervin. Strangely enough, during this whole Mad Hatter time, I kept in touch with Yvonne. She couldn't contact me because I didn't have a permanent address for years at a time.

Whenever I did find the time to make the effort I could go to the Red Cross office at the local V.A., give them the info they needed and they would make the connection, somehow. I have to take my cap off to those people, they take care maximum bidness."

"You said that you had directed your V.A. Comp check to her, electronically, so they can always reach her by going into the computer."

"Damn, Willie man, I got to give it to you. You may be a writer, but you're still smart."

I could sense that he was on the verge of doing one of his "detours." I had to beat him to the punch.

"Twenty years into your heron addiction. Can you look back on especially memorable time, either good or bad, that you experienced during that time?"

He took a sip of his tea; leaned back in his seat and stared up at the ceiling so long I thought he had forgotten my question.

"Willie, to tell you the honest to God truth, I have to say, all I can recall is twenty years of bad experiences, purely negative shit. Every day was a bad experience, some more bad than others, but nothing good. No, not ever. That is, unless you could say that being able to score for your fix was a 'good' experience?"

"How did you kick? How did you break the monkey's grip on your back?"

He smiled at me, an unusual gesture for him.

"I like that. I like that ... 'monkey's grip on your back'. How did I do it? Here's the truth. A friend of mine, we all need friends like this; my friend whispered 'a little known secret' in my ear – 'hey man, one way to keep that monkey off your back is to drink it off.'"

"What did he mean by that?"

"Get drunk. That's what that meant. Like, you could start pouring booze down your throat and you would forget about the monkey. Since I was desperate, I was sick of the dope fiend cycle – shoot up - nod out - hunt for more heron - shoot up - nod out – hunt! I was tired of the cycle, so I went for the wine.

Richard's Wild Irish Rose is as strong as bourbon, Scotch, any of 'em. And it was much cheaper. So, I started drinking pints of this rot gut wine. It lasted for about three – four days, this substitute grati-fication thing. 'Til I discovered the combination of Wild Rose with heron was, how shall I put it? Delightful. So, off I go into Wino/Heron hell."

"What was that like?"

I almost bit my tongue off, asking the question, but I felt I had no choice. If I was going to write an honest book, I have to put as much truth into it as I could.

"The wino/heron hell ...."

I was beginning to see Rufus as a world class actor. He seemed to have a wagon load full of facial expressions, dozens of tonalities for whatever he wanted to say, in whatever way he wanted to say it. He used his super sad tone for this.

"My personal wino/heron hell. Under the influence of the heron I trotted from one place to another, hunting for the bread to cop that fix. Now, with this need to stay drunk when I wasn't high, I sort of lurched/staggered around. I added ten more years onto my time in wino/heron hell …."

"Rufus, you're talking about a thirty-year trip?"

"That's exactly what it was – a trip. And I have to tell you that most of what happened during that time was a blur to me. It's still like a blur. I can flash back at strange scenes from time-to-time, that are clear as water, for a short time and then it's gone."

"Give me an example."

Deep inhalation, slow exhalation. His eyes closed for a few beats. The scene is set.

"I felt like I was coming back to life. Or maybe I was being born again. I couldn't really figure out which. I blinked up into this bright white light. I looked around. I was laying on a gurney in a hospital room. I gripped the sides of the gurney trying to get a grip on myself. Three men in scrubs were standing on the right side of the gurney. One of the guys in scrubs had a clipboard and he was talking to the other two.

My senses cleared up for me to recognize that I was in a hospital, these were doctors and they were talking about me.

'They're not holding the driver, he has witnesses that say this guy ran out into the street from between two parked cars, put a helluva dent into the side of this car ….'

I slipped over the left side of the gurney and I was half way to the door before they noticed ….

'Hey! Come back here! You've got a fractured ankle!'

It was a County Hospital, a lobby full of people. I was hopping and skipping out of the front door before they really got started. Thank God I was on the 1st floor, I would never have made it down some steps. Want another example? I got dozens, if I can remember 'em."

"What kind of treatment did you get for your fractured ankle?"

It was sad little sound he made, in sync with the sad tone of the story.

"Treatment? I made it over to Chi Chi's place, one of my fellow dope fiends who used to let me sleep on the floor in her bathroom sometimes. She tied my right ankle up real tight with a couple of her stockings."

"That was the treatment?"

"That was the treatment she gave me and then put me out because she had 'bidness' to take care of. I got lucky later on that night when I hip hopped past somebody who had left his garage door open for a few seconds. Lord in heaven! A ten speed! I hopped on and pedaled away like I had discovered gold.

Later that night, after I had busted into somebody's car and grabbed a whole armful of clothes somebody had just got out of the cleaners …."

"Never leave stealable stuff in your car."

"You got that right, Willie man. I pedaled straight to Big Bun's shootin' gallery to cop. I had clothes to sell. I sold the clothes, had enough bread to party a bit. I had been on the scene about a couple hours, sprawled out on my bike, to keep the other dope fiends from stealing it. One of the dudes sprawled out on this dilapidated sofa across from me says …

'Hey, Mel, why yo' ankle all swoll up like that?'

I looked down and sure enough my left was fat as a watermelon. Chi Chi had tied up the wrong ankle. We all had a big laugh tying the stockings on the right ankle. And then shot up some more heron."

"When did you get treatment? You know, your ankle put in a cast and all that?"

"Never happened, pal. I just self-medicated and let Nature take its course."

CHAPTER 15

"I just cannot make myself believe what this beast monster is saying, the lies he's telling ...."

"ZiZi, ZiZi baby, calm down ... just keep in mind what these thirty-seven psychiatrists and mental health experts told us in 'The Dangerous Case of Donald Trump'."

"I haven't read that, I've just seen his niece talk about his neurotic ass."

"She's cool, but these thirty-seven, originally twenty-seven shrinks, were out there, back in 2017, way before Mary Trump started revealing her insights. This book, edited by Bandy X. Lee, M.D., M.Div., Assistant Clinical Professor in Law and Psychiatry at the Yale School of Medicine.

Degrees at Yale, interned at Bellevue, Chief Resident at Mass. General, Research Fellow at Harvard Medical School.

Also a Fellow of the National Institute of Mental Health. Worked in several maximum-security prisons, co-founded Yale's Violence and Health Study Group, leads a violence prevention collaborators group for the World Health Organization. Has written more than one hundred reviewed articles, edited academic books, and is the author of the textbook 'Violence'."

"Willie, sounds like you've just read the bio-blurb from 'The Dangerous Case of Donald Trump'."

We were having a little fun, tele-zooming each other from 'Frisco to El-A', I had just finished a session with Rufus, so I was in touch.

"You got that exactly right, I just read you the bio-blurb of this woman who said; 'Listen! Y'all, I know we're not supposed to reveal psychiatric secrets and all such as that. But, we have to suspend some norms, and warn you – This motherfucker is nuts.' Well, when you read the book you'll understand a whole lot more about who the 'beast monster' really is.'"

"Willie, I hear you loud 'n clear, but how do you explain, how do these thirty-seven shrinks explain the appeal that this beast monster has for so many millions, millions of people?"

"ZiZi, correction, say so many millions of <u>White</u> folks. That's going to be one of the big questions I'm going to put to Rufus when we get together tomorrow. Or maybe the next day after tomorrow...."

"The brother's playing Diva on you, huh?

"No, no, no, nothing like that. It's just about a certain kind of rhythm. If it's time that we go 'there', then that's where we'll be, otherwise, it comes off in an off-rhythm way. I have to adjust myself to his rhythm, simple as that. I'll talk to him about this White folks appeal for the 'beast monster'."

We continued for a while, most of it might be considered semi-porno, but we didn't do it that way. In any case, at the end we agreed on a number of points, and that signaled the beginning of our marriage, long range.

We decided to do it at the ocean.

"Awright, brother Rufus, two days ago, when we last got together ...."

"I know, I know, I missed a day, please don't whip me, master Willie." A fake cringe to the left.

We had our masks off, sitting at opposite ends of one of those stone picnic tables they have at the crest of a hill in Bixby Park, overlooking the Pacific.

He played me so pitifully well, he made me feel that I was ragging <u>his</u> ass if <u>he</u> missed a day with me.

"C'mon, Rufus, you know I'm not on your case. I'm just keeping stuff on track."

He nodded in agreement, I think. The big beautiful, soft white flecked waves, the Pacific. It almost seemed a shame to be delving into all of this horrible shit on such a beautiful day. Did I mention that I had brought a small notebook and a couple ballpoints with me? I was beginning to feel a need for notes on the spot.

"So, let's get back to you tripping around with a fractured left ankle, self-medicating, letting Nature take its course."

"Yeahhh, you got it right, all of it."

"And you say you went thru ten years of this, this kind of scene? Plus the twenty-heron time?"

"Yessir, you got that correct. Thirty blurred wind tossed dodo splattered Heron slobbery kinky farted yearning-fix fix fix-years. Plus the wino com-ponent. Just goes to show you how much a human being's body and psyche can take.

Under the influence of both heron and alcohol, I can remember waking up in the middle of a city street, cars detouring around my body, like I was a large boulder in the middle of a small stream."

The image of this scene froze my imagination in place. I tried to flee past the scene, but I couldn't. Traffic ran over people, it didn't detour around them. And here was someone telling me that they had lain down in the middle of the street and survived.

"So, how did you manage escape being killed?"

"Good question, Willie. I woke up, realized where I was and eased off the scene."

"Easy as that, huh?"

"Well, here I am."

He opened the spidery arms on his narrow frame and gave me a broad smile, an unusually broad smile. I noticed that he had a few missing teeth on the top and bottom. It was kind of a Halloween pumpkin effect. But joyful, not sad.

"Bottom line, Mr. Rufus, suh, how did you get off this heron-wino merry-go-round?"

"You want the Instant Noodle explanation, huh?"

I took notice, once again, that he was always trying to put me on the spot, on the defensive. I was at *Stage One* of learning how to defend myself, my perimeters.

"Rufus, if the Instant Noodle explanation works for you, it's alright with me. It's your story, my brother."

I was getting to him, I could feel it in my backbones, my vertebrae, because they resonated when the truth was being played.

"Hey, Willie, don't get wolf-man on me, o.k.? I'm gonna tell you the utter profound truth, o.k.?"

"That's all I'm asking you for, that's all I'm asking you for."

"Concerning the heron-wino merry-go-round thing? I think the first trickle/movement happened when I stood in front of this old White guy with the snow white hair who informed me in a fairly matter-of-fact-way that he was putting me in jail for ten years.

Ten years in jail for a frame-up."

"You were framed for a ten-year sentence?"

"Yes, that's what it was. I'm not going to take you thru all of the dreary details. But what happened is that this corrupt cop and this threatened drug dealer had collaborated. The cop told the dealer – 'You're going up for time, unless you can throw me some red meat.' And that's what they did. The drug dealer gave me a kilo of Colombo heron to deliver to whatshisname and they pulled me over in the middle of the transaction.

I saw what the situation was right from the Git. And I understood what I had to do. I had to do my time. I had allowed myself to be played and I had to pay for that, and I did, in San Quentin. Ever been in a maximum security prison, Willie?"

"Yes, I have. I taught a creative writing class under the auspices of a program called Out Reach, from 1988-1990. Yeah, I've been in San Quentin."

Rufus settled back very slowly in the sand dune behind him, softly muttering – "Well, I'll be got damned; well I'll be got damned...."

I don't really think that the brother felt that I was going to do a real story of Rufus until we got to the San Quentin part. This is what he told me.

Rufus in San Quentin

"First thing you have to remember about me being in San Quentin is my size. Standing straight up in my bare feet, I was 5 feet four inches tall. Seems like I've shrunk an inch over the years, but I guess that's age."

"Yeah, it's true, we shrink as we grow older."

He sneered at me and didn't have to say it – what the hell do you know about growing older, young ass punk? He leavened his sneer with a sarcastic smile, took a sip of his tea and took me into his life in San Quentin.

"The reason I mention my size was because it really mattered in San Quentin. Five feet four inches tall, one hundred and twenty pounds. I found out, weeks later, that a bunch of predators had sat around, playing cards to decide who was going to be 'my man'.

Just think about this, Willie man, you got four or five dudes who look like Congolese gorillas, sitting around, gambling on who was gonna be the first to penetrate your round eye, your body, your soul.

What they didn't know about me would've filled up a couple books. A tough little cookie from the nut busting Westside of Chicago. A tunnel rat in Viet Nam. I was afraid, but not panicky. I knew, in order to survive in that environment, I had to become a little bit crazy, at the same time remain sane.

It happened exactly one week after I finished my quarantine time and was released into the general population. It took exactly five days for it to happen; one of the Congolese gorillas came up behind me in the chow line and pressed his dick up against my back. It felt like an iron pipe or something.

I turned around, took careful aim, and punched his dick with all my Hap Ki Do strength. I released a great Ki eye! As I punched. This guy's dick was so hard I thought I had hurt my fist punching it. I would never be able to describe the satisfaction I got from hearing this would be predator scream! SCREAM!

I hurt him bad, Willie, you know what I'm saying?"

"I know what you're saying, Rufus, then what?"

"They conducted an 'investigation of the incident' and determined that I was guilty of 'assault of a fellow convict'. Or something like that.

I can't recall the exact wording of the charge, but it entitled me to do thirty days in the Hole, in solitary confinement.

The Hole was in a prison underneath the prison, a real dungeon. It was a place where people went crazy on a regular basis. I saw it for what it was the first time. It was a soul breaker, a torture. It took me about thirty hard minutes to determine what I had to do.

I went into my tunnel rat mode of thinking, with a little mythical help from my ol' tunnel rat partner, 'Mr. Strings.' We were locked in for twenty-three hours and let out for an hour of 'exercise.' I refused to go out for the 'exercise' for the first week of my stay in the Hole because I was afraid that the gorilla man had put out a hit on me."

I have to confess, I was really glad that he paused. It gave me time to take a deep breath, to release it slowly, to try to keep my normal in charge. After his pause, he carried on, just as easy as you please. The whole thing seemed totally crazy to me. We were out on the beach, out on the beautiful beach, with the beautiful ocean in front of us. And here is the brother rolling all of this horrible shit out at me.

"I was given my second test, a couple days after I got out of the Hole. You're always being tested in the joint. Every day is a test of survival. My second-would-be predator was found in his cell with his throat slashed from ear to ear."

"You killed him?"

"That's not what I said, my friend. I said that he was found in his cell with his throat slashed from ear to ear. The police couldn't prove that I had done it, but they decided to give me 90 days in the Hole, just on G.P. I call that my second test.

Once again, I went into my tunnel rat mode. I made myself, I made myself become very, very still for long periods of time. I laid on this futon type mattress on this stone platform and thought … I know, you want to know what I thought?"

Of course I wanted to know what he thought, but I didn't even know how to frame the question.

"There were times when I just laid there and thought about the Entire present, where I was, what happening around me. On a number of occasions, I laid up there and recalled the time of my birth."

"'C'mon, Rufus, don't shit me, man."

He placed both hands in a cross on his heart, a plea for me to believe what he was saying, without a word being spoken. I had to back off from my skepticism.

"From the time of my birth. I remembered the moment, the time when I was expelled from my mother's womb. It was definitely a shock, believe me. Here I am, coming from this deliciously warm place into this big, bright cold world. Remember, I was born in Chicago, and I don't care what anybody says – if you're born in Chicago, even in the summertime, it's cold."

Fellow Chicagoans, we laughed at his statement. Chicago, the Almighty Hawk, that wind that blows around a corner, up into your pants and curdles your nuts. The Almighty Hawk. Yeah, I could relate to that. He had one on me. I couldn't recall the time I was birthed, but I could recall the Hereafter.

"I might've missed a few minutes of the after birth, but it didn't take me long to catch up to a bunch of after moments. Dig where I'm comin' from, Willie?"

"I hear you, Rufus, I hear you."

"Then I was doing what I had to do to survive. You are not allowed a whole lot of time to get your shit together, if you're born in the ghetto. It was like I could recall each moment that I needed to survive, like infusing yourself with energy. A special kind of energy.

It was really hard when I heard the faint sound of a cellie, down there in this dungeon, who had given it up, had collapsed into madness. And, I can recall, I had only become eight/ten years old in my imagination.

I discovered Imagination in the Hole. I settled into Moments that allowed me to focus on Moments. Times when I had lived. Some of what I hallucinated. That's mostly what it was, I think. But I can't say that in any kind of definite way.

All in all, I wound up spending five years in the Hole. It wasn't a year by year thing. I had a few months of breaks in between. When I look back on it, I have to be honest and say, maybe I did a bunch of shit to get myself sent to the Hole. Don't get me wrong, Willie, the Hole was the Hole.

Meanwhile, when I wasn't in the Hole, I was in the Library. Or I was in some kind of class. I took this speech class three times. Concerning the Library; I learned how to speed read 'cause I was always afraid that somebody was going to snatch the book out of my hands."

"One question. Would you say that reading saved you in the joint?"

"Reading helped, but it was the Muslim Brotherhood that really saved me."

"How did that happen?"

"I became a Muslim. Nothing religious about my decision to convert, it was strictly a matter of survival. I had two strikes against me. The Congolese gorilla, the one I had sucker punched in the dick, definitely wanted a piece of me. And the friends of this dude who had his throat cut also wanted me too, 'cause they were convinced that I was guilty.

So, as soon as I could I applied for membership in the Brotherhood. Frankly, I think they were glad to bring me in. They wanted young bloods with Heart. And I had shown that I had Heart. It was definitely a mutual defense thing.

What everybody understood about the Muslim Brotherhood was two things. They didn't take no shit from nobody, not even from the police. They were respected. And if you messed over one of the Brotherhood, you had the whole Brotherhood to deal with.

I don't exactly know how many Brothers we had because there were a lot of Brotherhood sympathizers, Lots. I'm telling you, my ass wouldn't have been worth a plugged nickel, if I hadn't joined the Brotherhood."

We had just about reached the end of our thread for the day. Except for one more question.

"Rufus, I was talking to ZiZi recently …"

"Your lady?"

"Yeah, my lady. She asked me an interesting question. She asked me – why do you think so many White folks have fallen under the Trump spell? She calls him 'The beast monster'."

"That really is an interesting question. Let me think on it."

October 2020. It felt like the whole country was inside of some kind of turbine. The virus was burning thru, people were lining up to get food, the political scene was white hot – Trump again or Biden? -- The Nazis had re-surfaced, racism had been re-upholstered, so much shit was happening at the same time. People were babbling in tongues strolling down the streets – everywhere.

I sat at my writing desk, the same day that I had asked Rufus the question about White folks falling for the "beast monster's" game, and wrote one hundred times "Do not panic". One hundred times I wrote this and read it back to myself out loud after I finished. These three words became my mantra. Before I went to sleep at night I said it. When I woke up I said it. And, at different times during the day.

I was determined to do two things before the end of the year, in order to start 2021 in good form, in high gear. Finish getting all of what I needed from Rufus, in order to write "Conversations" in a way that would be appealing to a lot of people. And number two, clear all of the negative truth out of my head, out of my life, so that I could receive the woman I loved, my precious ZiZi, with a clean slate.

CHAPTER 16

"Hey, lookahere, Big Shot, why don't we get a couple burgers and get on back over to the beach?"

"You like the ocean, don't you?"

"Always did. I remember going to Da Nang ..."

"What's that? Sounds Viet Namese."

"Willie, you are so im-patient. Yeah, Da Nang was sort of like an R and R resort in 'Nam. It was almost as though you were in another world for a couple hours, or maybe a couple days. Well, it seemed like that. No war anywhere close."

We strolled down the beach a bit, to what had become our "conference spot". Beautiful October day in California. Hard to believe that the country, right behind our sand dune, was on fire, literally.

"So, what about these White folks; you said you wanted to think on it."

He turned his snarky look my way, sipping from his jumbo coke.

"You think I was lying to you?"

Uhh ohh... be careful, don't let him lure you into one of his Rufus cul d' sacs.

"No sir, I know you would never lie."

"Willie, quit! You talk mo' shit than a Thanksgiving turkey. You know me by now, you know when I say I'm going to do something it's a done deal. Now then, having said that, which is what everybody is saying these days, let me give you my spin on this. I've almost pinned it down to about four things, maybe five.

Number one, Donald Trump is a White man. You have to understand what that means, for real. In the same way that most human beings think that they are superior to all of the animals on the Earth, which makes us human supremacists. Dig where I'm going?"

"Almost, don't stop 'til you get there."

"Don't be trying to tell me what to do!"

Yep, then it was that bipolar flare up. I simply nodded neutrally.

"Trump, as a White man in America, which means, for millions of White people, that he is <u>supposed</u> to be the Alpha dog in this country, if not in the whole world. They believe this, like some folks believe in the Bible or the Koran. And the basis for that belief is that the man is White. That's one of the reasons why they're willing to go to his Covid19 spreader rallies, why they ignore his lies. He is the absolute best pathological liar of our time. They ignore his criminal behavior, all of the garbage because he is a White man."

"Rufus, are you saying all White people in America?"

"Willie, my brother, read my lips. I'm saying White people period. When or if you can ever get that jive ass White liberal to admit the bone dry truth, he'll reveal that he believes in the White man thing too."

I felt tempted to argue the point, but I chilled. I didn't want to inhibit his flow.

"He takes a crap and smears their faces in it and they eat it up. I think, for him, he came along at exactly the right time."

He paused to slurp up the rest of his coke. He had found his groove. I could relax.

"Think about this, Willie Writer, if you will. Can you think of any Black person, especially a Black male, or a Brown person, or a Native American, or an Asian of any type, who could blunder from one scandal to the next, who could run all of the games that "the beast monster" – is that what your lady calls him?"

"Exactly that."

"And still be sitting on the White Stool? I think not. That's what makes me say all White folks. If the White people had wanted to shut his shit down, in the beginning, they could've done it because, as you know, White folks in America are Very Powerful.

I don't want to hear no bullshit about Demo-crats and Re-publicans, when it comes to what I'm talking about. Am I making you late for a date, or something?"

133

"Rufus, stop trying to play on me. I'm getting tired of this shit." I really meant it. Rufus a.k.a. Melvin Montaigne Dixon III, an astute observer of the human thing … felt that I was becoming pissed off at this play on my psyche. He switched to cool immediately.

So, as I was saying, as I just explained – White was/is right for millions of Whites in America. This is point two of what I'm talking about. As much as White people in America hate to acknowledge this fact; undercurrent racism has always been a driving force behind every damned thing White America has ever been about.

Check it out; these Europeans found their way over here, killed all the Native Americans they could find, enslaved all of the Africans they could catch, excluded as many Asians as they could, and claimed that they had discovered this place because they had superior fire power.

You see, Willie, that was the thing that made them 'White Men'. Being 'White' meant that you considered everybody else inferior to all people who were White. This has been re-enforced so much over the years that you have millions of these White people who believe their own propaganda. You understand what I'm saying?"

"I think it would be pretty hard <u>not</u> to understand. But let me ask you this – how long will this White Man Syndrome last?"

He sifted the sand thru his fingers, something he did when he was giving serious thought to something.

"You know something, man, I've given this a lot of thought years ago when these young White people helped me get outta San Quentin three years before my official release date …"

"You didn't tell me about that."

"I was going to have to, sooner or later. Yeah, that's what happened. These people belonged to something called the Innocence Project. They went around digging into prison files and stuff like that, to find people who had been un-justly convicted. When they got to my case, they told me that I shouldn't've been convicted in the first place.

I definitely agreed with them. And after about six months of yanging-yanging back and forth I was released."

"How much time…?"

"I had done seven years."

"I'd like to hear more about what they did to get you released, but let me go back to my question, how long will this White man Syndrome last?"

"I used to think that it would be over during my life time. You know, during the sixties. But then I started looking at things with realistic eyes and I had to conclude this shit ain't <u>never</u> going to end. Let me put a couple stipulations on that. It may end when the last White man is dead. Or when some really and truly courageous White people put in the kind of work needed to get them and the rest of their folks outta 'jail'."

"You see it like that?"

"Yeahhh, that's the way I see it. Millions of White folks are locked up behind racial walls. Some of them have been locked in by circumstances beyond their control.

Others have locked themselves in because they're desperately afraid that we're going to treat them the way they treated us, when we get into the power seat. Both of these groups need to have some good lawyers on their case."

Rufus turned his face away from me. Was he smiling or crying?

🌿

I spent a hard hour or two puzzling over his White man Syndrome theory. Casually, I wanted to dismiss the whole thing, 'til I started doing some serious thinking. I had to admit, he had a point. White folks in America, after all of the pain and misery they had inflicted on people of color, should be fearful of how they would be treated when we occupied the power seat. But how could I say that to them, without sounding racially offensive? -- People of color would never behave like y'all have behaved. There's no history anywhere of colored people slaughtering White people, just because they were White. Or enslaving White people just because they were White. Or discriminating against White people on a national level, just because they could.

I felt a real urge to get back to Rufus about this, and a whole bunch of other stuff. I was beginning to really feel that I had an interesting can of worms in my notebook.

No Rufus. My third day of being in the Mall parking lot waiting for Melvin Montaigne Dixon III to appear.

No Rufus. I really felt vulnerable. What if he had decided to just say, that's it, that's all, to Hell with it. I really felt that he could do something like that.

I checked the time. One p.m. His "work schedule" was from eleven to two (11:00 – 2 pm), he had made that absolutely clear. I was thirty seconds away from driving away when this woman, one of the resident members of the Likka Sto' parking lot gang, moved toward me, gesturing for me to wait a minute.

Strangely, she was the only member of the gang on the scene at that moment. I had no idea where the rest of the members were. It didn't matter all that much. This heavy set woman, middle aged, full up front and ample behind, reminded me of my Aint Mamie. That was the way I always referred to her – Aint Mamie. The game started the minute she huffed-puffed up to the passenger side of my car. She had a bright mask on, otherwise I would've double clutched off the scene.

"Honey, you looking for Rufus, huh?"

I nodded yes. I wanted to see what the deal was.

"Well, let me ask you this … could you help me out? I can tell you some information about Rufus."

I looked at her eyes. I remembered her telling me the difference between Drug Sto' Rufus and my man, Likka Sto' Rufus. There was something about her earnest approach.

"What kind of information?"

"Like I said, could you help me out?"

I felt powerful and greedy at the same time I had something she wanted and she had something I wanted, maybe.

"What do you want?"

It wasn't hard to guess, her hands were trembling on the open window of my car. She wanted a drink.

"Uhh, I just wanted to buy myself a lil' taste, that's all. My check is late and …."

I didn't want to hear the whole sorry ass story.

"And you say you have something to tell me about Rufus?"

"Yessir, I do."

I hated hearing her say that, this middle aged woman. She was probably old enough to be my grandmother.

As luck would have it, I had three twenty dollar bills in my pocket. I gave her one. I could see that alky gleam light up her eyes before she shuffled off to Mr. Kim's for her fix.

What could she tell me that I didn't already know? A few minutes later she shuffled back over to the car, patting her scrappy looking diddy bag.

"What did you get?"

"Oh, I bought a pint of CO'vosea. I like a little 'nac when I can afford it."

I had to smile. Here was a dedicated cheap wine drinker telling me that she liked cognac when she could afford it. O well....

"So, what do you want to tell me?"

"Could we go somewhere else? I wouldn't wanna have Moses and the rest of 'em see us talkin'."

Damn, this was becoming complicated, just what I didn't need. But I was curious. What the hell ...

"Where to?"

"Signal Hill ain't too far."

"O.k., Signal Hill, but I don't have much time. You sit in back and don't take your mask off."

"That's cool, I understand."

I opened my window and rolled the passenger window down. I wanted to have as much ventilation in the car as possible. If I had heard her cough one time I would've stopped the car and put her out. Signal Hill, a few blocks east on Pacific Coast, a left turn on Cherry, north to Skyline Drive, a right turn up the hill to Signal Hill.

Nice day to be on the Hill. She was half way out of the car the minute I parked.

"Be right back."

I got out and watched her hurry to get to the ladies. I felt for her, she had to guzzle a few swallows "to calm her nerves". It took her a couple minutes. Just a few old duffers walking around, little ol' ladies walking their little dogs.

137

"C'mon, we can sit at the table over there and take off our masks, if we sit at opposite ends of the table. There's a nice breeze, so we don't have to worry about infecting each other."

"You know all about this viruses 'n stuff, huh?"

"Not everything, just what I read and what the health care people tell us."

We took our positions, properly spaced on opposite sides of this stone picnic table, and took off our masks. Funny thing happened when the pandemic hit and the intelligent people started wearing masks, it became a sort of unusual surprise to see the whole face.

"Uhh, what's your name, Mrs.?"

"Annette Glover, but for some reason everybody call me 'Molly'."

"Molly, my name is Willie."

"I know. Willie, I got a medium sized Coca Cola cup, you mind if I pour this, CO'voseya into this cup? That way, if the police come up on us, we won't have no bottle."

"I think that's smart, Molly, a smart thing to do."

I watched her dip her hand into her diddy bag and do a slick tilt of the pint bottle of Covoisier into her cup. She was smooth. A pleasant looking, nut brown skinned face, about sixty something. She probably looked the same way she looked when she was much younger, except for the soggy effect of the alcohol on her features.

"Be right back …."

She shuffled away to toss the empty pint bottle into a nearby trash can.

"Police be messin' with folks about drinkin' in the parks and what not."

It was easy to guess that her deep Southern accent meant one of the ex-Confederate states, but I didn't want to get into linguistics.

"You wanted to tell me something about Rufus?"

She took a water glass swallow of her 'nac and looked off into the distance before she spoke.

"Rufus playin' long con on you, honey."

"What makes you think that?"

"I know that for a fact, that's what he do."

I'm sure I must have stared at her face for a full minute, trying to figure what to think about what she had just said. Long con. I knew enough about the games to understand what she had just dropped on me. She took a smaller swallow from her cup, staring into my eyes.

"He ask you for any money to go see his wife and sons in Australia yet? You know, dry beg on you?"

Miss Molly was obviously a bit tipsy now, but there was the ring of truth in her question.

"No, not yet. But you know it's hard for me to believe that he's making all this stuff up about being a tunnel rat in Viet Nam and all the rest."

"Why you say that? He got a good brain in his head just like you do. You make up stuff too, don't you?"

She was passing the cup to me before I reached for it. I didn't sip, I took a full Molly swallow. To hell with germs.

"Please, don't stop now, I'd like to hear more of this."

"Well, what else you want me to say?"

"How does he pick the people he wants to play on?"

"Rufus slick, he don't pick the mark, he let the mark pick him. You understand what I'm sayin'?"

"I'm not sure, run it down to me."

"Awright, lemme give you an example. This ol' White man shows up at the Likka Sto'. Ol' White man, you know the type—so wrinkled up and White …. Look like they been wrung out and hung up to dry."

She obviously enjoyed seeing me smile, but she wasn't overjoyed to see me take another big sip from the cup. I put her anxiety at ease.

"Molly, don't worry. We can take my change from this first pint and I'll add the rest for another pint."

She nodded pleasantly, lit up.

"So, what happened with the ol' White man?"

I knew, from my Rufus time, that I had to keep her on the track.

"Well, you know how Rufus do people when they try to throw some spare change his way …."

"He won't accept that, he wants paper money, not metal money."

"That's exactly right. Now, you know that kinda freaks some folks out. A pan handler, a beggar man trying to set the terms of the deal. O no, no, no sirreee. But they come back 'cause they can't help theyself. That's what happened between Rufus and the ol' White man.

Just like with you we could see it happen right in front of our eyes. I don't know all of the details, but the way it was told to me was that he, Rufus, wanted to go back to Austria-lean to see his wife and son. Or some such thing as that.

Like I said, this is the way it was told to me. And he managed to come up with some kind of fairy tale that shook twenty-five hundred dollars outta the ol' White man's bank account."

On one level I just couldn't accept what she was saying to me. On the other hand I felt she was telling me the truth. How did she know about his wife and sons in Australia? I decided to use one question as the deciding factor.

"Molly, how do you know about this wife and sons thing in Australia thing?"

She took a long sip from her cup before answering.

"You know how men is, when they done had a few."

"But Rufus doesn't drink."

"You right about that, he don't drink now. But if you brag on what you done did to people who <u>do</u> drink, then the word gets out."

I almost had to wrestle the cup out of her hand to take another sip of the cognac. I was thunder struck by what I was hearing. You mean to tell me that this guy is making, has made up all of this stuff?

"Molly, why do you think he comes up with this wife and some foreign country stuff?"

"I don't' know, tell ya the truth. But I can tell you this much – it works, you got to remember, Rufus been doing what he been doing for a long while, all up 'n down.

All up and down Cali-fornia. He don't go up too far north 'cause he don't like the cold too much so, maybe I should say, he go from here down to San Diego and back a lot."

"And you're telling me that he pulls this scam off in San Diego too?"

"That's what I been told. Why wouldn't he do what he's doin' in different places? If you figure out something that's working for you, why stay in one place?"

The cognac, just enough in my empty stomach to give me a slight buzz. The thought circled around in my head. Truth is stronger than fiction, much stronger.

"Willie," I was pleased to hear her call me by my name without sounding deferential; "honey, what you got to understand, if you gon' survive out here on these mean streets, you got to develop some street smarts. Rufus ain't really doing nothin' super special. I guess you could say that he done learnt how to lie better than most people."

She drained the cup as we stood up to leave. She was drunk, but not sloppy drunk. I was tempted to ask her a few questions about herself, but cancelled the thought. I had enough on my plate already. We pulled our masks on as we approached the car.

"Molly, what made you decide to tell me about Rufus?"

I thought she hadn't heard my question. I repeated it as we positioned ourselves in the car, her in the back seat, far right, and me behind the wheel.

"I heard you the first time. I can't rightfully put my finger on the reason. Maybe it's got something to do with being a Christian woman. I was pretty deep in the church before I got drunk."

She made the statement in such a matter of fact way. I looked up at her face in the rear view mirror. Her eyes were glittering like marbles, like she wanted to cry but couldn't.

"Yeahhh, before I got drunk, I paid strict attention to what was right and what's wrong. My Momma and Daddy put that in me. So, I guess I just feel bad when I see people trying to do other people wrong. You know, when you out here in these streets, you see so much dirt goin' down you get used to it.

That ain't happened to me, I still know right from wrong. Look, why don't you let me off in the middle of the block? It wouldn't do me no good for Moses and the others to see me with you."

"I understand."

I slipped her a twenty as she was getting out of the car.

"Oh, honey, you don't have to give me this."

"You can give it back to me if you don't want it."

She gave me an affectionate pat on my shoulder as she made her exit.

"Willie, you a rascal, you know that?"

"If you say so, Miss Molly."

I drove away from her feeling like I had just spent an hour with one of my favorite Aints.

CHAPTER 17

Next Day

I drove past the mall at 1:45, Rufus time. There he was, in his position. I drove into the far side of the parking lot, parked. And sat there studying the main character in "Conversations".

Talk about mixed emotions. What if Molly had told me a lie about Rufus? For what reason? To get a drink. What if Rufus was just feeding me some stuff he had made up? Well, if it was made up stuff, it was pretty good stuff.

The only big problem I could see had to do with the genre I would put it in the autobiography of Rufus with Willie West. The Willie West biography of Rufus. "The Big Lie", as told by Rufus to naïve Willie West. I decided that it would be best to put all of those concerns on hold for a while, until I had probed a bit more deeply into what was happening.

"'He asks you for any money to go see his wife and sons in Austria-lean yet? You know, dry beg on you?'"

Molly's questions forced me to do a whole montage of flashbacks. He had never asked me for money, directly, and had never dry begged, so far as I could recall.

Dinners at the Salamat Po and the Vietnamese Pho American, my idea. I felt satisfied with what was happening between us. I was content to continue to follow the vibe, to see what was going to go down.

The first thing he called out when I drove toward him – "Hey Willie! Where you been at, brother?!"

I parked again, this time closer to the Salamat Po. It was ten after two.

"You want to talk about it over some chicken adobo?" I had decided to keep careful track of my offers.

"Hell, yeah! I love that chicken 'dobo!"

Lola welcomed us with her usual dance-like body language. I don't think I've ever seen somebody so graceful.

"Your table is ready." Great. I would have a chance to study, to read Rufus's expressions as we talked. He seemed to be unusually animated. He was the first to order. Was he scamming me for a dinner?

I had to push petty paranoia aside. He would have to be about more than some chicken. You can't fatten your bank account with chicken adobo.

"I'll have that chicken adobo, Miss Lola, I don't know what he's going to have." Pointing at me.

Like I said, he was unusually animated.

"I'll have the fish stew and tea."

"I'll have the tea too."

After giving our orders, we had a moment of quiet before he opened up on me.

"Guess what? Willie … I just got four letters from Yvonne and the boys."

My scam antennae shot up to one hundred and ten. I couldn't help but be a little sarcastic. I wanted to see how he would take it.

"Haven't seen you in a few days, I thought maybe you had tripped off to Australia …"

He turned his charm button on.

"Yeahhh, I know, I went to A.W.O.L. on you. But I'm back now and here's what happened. I tripped over to the V.A. to keep this appointment and the Red Cross had left these four letters with my primary care Doctor, in Charley Unit. Four letters from Yvonne and the boys."

He flashed the four envelopes at me, like a deck of cards, with his hand covering the stamps. What could I say? Let me see those. This was becoming very, very interesting.

"So, what're they saying? They miss you?"

The chicken adobo and fish stew were placed in front of us.

"Bon appetit" Lola said in a sexy voice.

"My goodness, Miss Lola, I didn't know y'awl spoke French."

She danced away smiling. That's what her movement said – I'm smiling.

The fish stew was delicious, as usual. And I could tell that Rufus was enjoying his chicken adobo. After a few satisfying bites we were ready to start talking.

"Well, Willie man, in answer to your question, as a matter of fact, they are missing me. As a matter of fact, they want to see me. Just think about it, man, I got two sons, one that I've never seen. Yvonne has sent me photos of herself and the boys over the years, but what's a photograph? No substitute for being there, for that personal contact."

I couldn't quite figure out where this was going, what I was supposed to say. I opted for a neutral – "Yeah, you got that right, there is no substitute for that personal contact."

A few spoons of fish stew later, I decided to get us back on <u>our</u> track.

"Rufus, I don't want to …."

"I know, I know, you want to get back to the story."

"I do, I have no choice. Either you finish what you begin, or you're not a real writer. That's what one of my writing teachers used to say."

He slouched in his seat, obviously disappointed at not being able to continue rapping about his wife and sons.

"Yeah, I hear you, Willie – so, where are we?"

"We left off when you were released from San Quentin, with the help of the Innocence Project people. What happened after that?"

We had settled into our usual question-answer format, except for me having a steno pad to take notes on.

"Willie, looks like you getting serious, my man."

I nodded in agreement, playtime was over.

Lola placed a fresh pot of tea on our table. She was almost an accessory to our collaboration.

"Well, to get right down to the nitty gritty, I have to say, honestly, that there wasn't a whole lot that happened. It took the lawyers about six months to get me a few peanuts from the state, for 'unjust incarceration,' or whatever they called it. I sent Yvonne a little money, but mostly I spent the rest on relapses."

"You went back on dope?"

145

"C'mon, man, don't say it like that. You sound so, so judgmental. What you have to remember is simply this – once a dope fiend, always a dope fiend."

I had heard enough about the dope fiend life style to know that it was hustle-get dope-shoot up-nod off. And repeat. Nothing really interesting or exciting about that. Or maybe I had missed something. I decided to probe a bit.

"Give me a taste, an example of something that happened to you, in between the time you got out of jail and when we met."

"You met me, I didn't meet you."

"Whatever. Can you think of something?"

He did his usual space-face think for a few beats.

"Yeah, I can think of something. It happened when I met this woman …"

I'm sure that my ears must've perked up a bit. This was an area we hadn't explored.

"I don't want you to get your sex pimples aroused or nothing like that, you have to remember – at the time, I was a loyal husband to – heron. That's right, lady Heron. That was my love, my sensation, my thang."

"I get it, Rufus, I get it. I spent years of my young life around dope fiends on the Southside of Chicago."

"Then you know what I'm talking about?"

"That's what I just said."

This guy could really exasperate me. There were moments when I felt like throwing something at him.

"So, for some reason, somehow, I wound up prowling around in Long Beach. I didn't know Long Beach from any place else, it was just another dope fiend 'grazing ground'. If you know what I mean?"

"I do know what you mean."

"Awright, we got that established. It was a dry time for me. I had gotten so fiendish and desperate, I was prowling thru neighborhoods, like this neighborhood, looking for something to steal, in broad day time.

Lo 'n behold, this African-American sister calls out to me from her front porch."

'Are you looking for some work?'

"Maybe it was the way she said it, you know, 'like can I help you?'"

"It took a hot minute for me to give her a fake – 'Uhh, yes, m'am, I'm looking for work.'"

"That's what happened. That was the beginning."

"What happened? What was the beginning?"

"That was the beginning of my relationship with the sister. Like I said to you, I was not out tom cattin', I was out looking for something to steal. She offered me the job of mowing her lawn and I took it. It was a funny kind of scene because it seems like the minute she pulled me in to do her lawn, three other sisters pulled me onto their lawns. It was honest work, but it was not exactly meeting my alcohol-drug agenda. Dig?"

"Dig..."

"I had to keep on stealing, in addition to mowing those lawns. I must've been one of the best conditioned dope fiend/drunks on the scene."

He paused with his narrative to curl his skinny arms up, in a muscle builder's pose. I almost laughed out loud.

"In addition, remember this. The sister who called on me was a devout Christian. It was like she had just finished reading her Bible about five minutes ago. It didn't take her long to figure out that I was a man with great dope needs.

We talked about it, in the backyard, when I was mowing, or nailing the back fence. She had enough sense not to let me go into the house, except to use the toilet that was right off the kitchen. I'm sure I would've found something to steal, if she had allowed me to get all the way into the place.

What I could see, just from glancing into the dining room, right off the kitchen, is that the place was thread bare. She was po' as a church mouse. Notice, I didn't say 'poor', I said 'po'."

"I gotcha!"

"Now, the way she scoped one of my bad habits came about when she caught me sucking on a pint of Wild Irish, just after I had mowed the back forty. You ever drink some Richard's Wild Irish Rose, Willie?"

"Rufus, gimme a fuckin' break. Every teen aged fool growing up in Chicago had to drink some of that terrible shit, at one time or another."

We exchanged affirmative high fives. We knew what we knew.

147

"Now, check this out. She calls to me, the second or maybe the third time she catches me 'Dick Smithing'. . . ."

"'Dick Smithing'? Seems like I've heard somebody say that before."

"It's from my generation, young Willie, means that you're sneaking to do something."

"Oh." What else could I say?

'Mr. Dixon, would you like to have some ice with that?'

"She was being nice, asking me in a civilized way, to stop chugalugging in her backyard."

"'Uhh, yes m'am', I accepted her offer of a glass filled with ice cubes. And, for some reason, off the top of my head, I asked her.

'It's a hot day, m'am, can I offer you some of this?'

'This ain't strong as that Jack Daniel's stuff my husband used to drink, is it?'

'O, no m'am, this is wine, it's not any way as strong as whisky.'

"So, that's the way it started. It got to the point, over the course of that summer ...."

"How long ago?"

"This happened about four years ago. It got to the point where she would have a fifth of the Wild Irish when I got there to hammer and nail a bit, mow the backyard. And I noticed that the fifth might be half full when she offered me a water glass full of ice and wine. I noticed that she was getting drunk on me.

Meanwhile, she's talking Gospel to me to get me 'off the needle', as she put it.

'Melvin, you've got to stop stickin' that needle in your body. We know that our Lord and Savior Jesus Christ caused wine to flow out of a rock, but there's nowhere in the Holy Bible that says He caused dope to come out of Nothin'."

"It was a really crazy time for me, Willie man, a really crazy time. When you have a devout person start talking to you, you have to listen. I listened, and I guess I was ready for the message 'cause I started doing a gradual withdrawal from my bad habits.

What you got to understand is that I didn't have a whole lot of help around me. I could go to the V.A. and try to get into one of the re-hab programs, but they were always completely surrounded by dope fiends."

I could only smile. I guess he couldn't see the irony of what he was saying.

"It was a helluva summer, believe me. I went cold turkey, on my own. I puked in public parks, I slept in ol' cars, I felt like I was freezing to death while sweat was pouring off of me like rainwater. I spent most of my nights sleeping up under the lifeguard stands over at the beach. I must've relapsed a dozen times. But gradually, very gradually, I grew stronger and stronger. Two weeks into my Hell, I went over to cut Miss Glover's lawn, shaking and trembling like a new born baby."

"What was her name?"

"Mrs. Glover."

"What was her first name?"

"Annette, Annette Glover. Most of the Likka sto' gang call her 'Molly', for some reason."

It felt like the blood was draining out of my head. Annette Glover, "Molly". Rufus didn't take notice of what went thru me, he was too deep in his story.

"They can call her whatever they want to call her, I'll always call her Mrs. Glover."

"Whatever happened to her?"

Yep, there it was once again, that spacey-face look. .

"You've seen her, she hangs out with Moses and the rest of them."

"What about you two, how do you get along?"

"We nod when we see each other. You have to remember, this is the person responsible for pulling me off the bottle and the needle. I'll always be grateful to her for that. She was the one who first told me that it would be better to beg than to steal. And I took her up on that."

"Do you feel a little guilty, maybe responsible for her being where she is today?"

"Not really. What you have to remember, Willie, is real simple – shit happens."

It probably took me about five minutes to call ZiZi and get into this story behind the story.

"Willie, let me clearly understand what you're telling me. You're telling me that this whole story Rufus has been telling you is something that he made up, that he is making up. Is that what you're saying?"

"Yeah, that's what I'm saying, but I can't really be certain. I mean I would have to do one of those Henry Gates' 'Find Your Roots' kind of things to really get at the truth."

It was a little bit unnerving to hear her start laughing. I let her laugh it out for a minute before I interrupted her.

"ZiZi, what's so funny, baby?"

"In a sense, this whole thing is funny-funny but not ha-ha funny. You know what I mean?"

The humor of it was beginning to climb up the back of my brain.

"I'm beginning to."

"Just think about it for a sec. You're the novelist, the writer of fiction and you wind up dealing with a guy who is telling you a story that's so far out, you can't decide if it's the truth or not … that's not just funny, it's deep."

"I'm afraid I have to agree with you."

"Oh, incidentally, talking about literary things, I've just had a conversation with Sally Abrams …."

"Doesn't ring a bell."

"She's the head of the Abrams, Hasoff and Wernick Agency."

"Oooo, you mean that agency?"

"That's the one. I told her about this latest book you're writing and she's very interested in reading your first fifty pages."

"How did you get thru to her? Agents at her level are pretty hard to reach."

"We do a lot of work for these people, so it's a two way street. We're always scratching each other's back, in one way or another. In any case, she'll be e-mailing you one day next week, to make her request legitimate."

"I'm looking forward to hearing from her. So, how're things going otherwise?"

"I'll be getting my drawers outta here the first week in December."

"I'm looking forward to seeing you, with or without your panties, uhhh, drawers."

"Willie, you are like a nasty lil/ boy, do you know that?"

"Is that why you love me?"

"For that and other reasons too. Look, I gotta run. Talk to you tomorrow."

"I love you, ZiZi."

"I love you too, Willie, 'bye."

"Bye."

I sat at my desk after we finished talking, my heart pounding against my chest. So this is what being in love feels like.

CHAPTER 18

Over the course of the following days I did a fine tooth comb search for anything in the "Conversations" manuscript that would work against me. I hadn't made an appointment to get together with Rufus after our last meeting, but I knew where I would be able to find him when I finished reviewing the first fifty pages of my manuscript.

Hollyweird, Anyone?

After a very careful review, I leaned back and asked myself, objectively; who in the hell would be interested in reading this? I came to the conclusion that it might be interesting to people who had never had a Rufus in their lives.

❦

A week went by. No Rufus. I drove thru at different times during his "shift." Eleven o'clock. No Rufus. Twelve thirty. No Rufus. One thirty. In between times I glued myself to my desk, to the "Conversations" manuscript. I wanted to be able to show him how our "Conversations" had given birth to a book.

[I had sent the first fifty pages to Ms. Sally Abrams, as requested in her e-mail – "*Zizi tells me that you have an unusual manuscript to send us. Please send the first fifty pages at your earliest convenience. We look forward to hearing from you.*

Sincerely, Sally Abrams]

Maybe I'm jumping the gun by saying I had a complete book, but I knew, if Sally Abrams said – "O.k. already, send the rest of it." … it would require only a few more pages to sew it up, to bring it to a conclusion.

Meanwhile, there were exchanges between me and ZiZi about love, life and the man she called, amongst other things; "beastmonster".

"Willie, did you hear/see what this beastmonster racist snake dog asshole narcissistic motherfucker did/said yesterday? No, he didn't say it, he tweeted it."

I grew to love listening to ZiZi rant about Trump. Her cussin' was eloquent, almost poetic –

"Think about what you would have to be, to snatch nursing babies from their mothers, to lock children up in cages, to ignore thousands of people dying from something you could've prevented. You know what …. I would call somebody that MEAN SPIRITED?"

"No, ZiZi, I don't know what you would call him. What would you call him?"

"I would call him a beastmonster snake dog sick ass cruel hyena motherfucker! That's what I would call him."

"Uhhh, ZiZi, could you repeat that?"

We usually dissolved in some form of hysterical laughter because she was never able to repeat what she had just exploded with.

"Willie, I just can't help myself sometimes. I have to turn off the T.V. when this ugly monster beast comes on. Don't get me wrong, I work in an office where they have some handsome, good looking

White men. So, it ain't about racial animosity, it's about looking at an evil monster motherfucker that's what he is. In addition to being a psychopath."

We focused on that psychopathic area for a long time because she had read the twenty seven-thirty-seven mental expert's opinion in "The Dangerous Case of Donald Trump" ("The Ramifications of Trump's Case is too serious to ignore. We must all speak up – before it's too late.") -- and agreed, understood what Dr. Bandy X. Lee, M.D., M. Div. was talking about.

"What's wrong with these stupid motherfuckers? These stupid **White motherfuckers**, to understand that their guy is crazy as hell. The motherfucker is Nuts! Can't they see that?!" I was somewhat shocked by her profanities.

"Yeah, baby, they can see it, understand it, but they are so attached to their White racial privilege-status that they would do anything, anything to retain that position in the world. ZiZi, sweetheart, you have to remember – the White folks in America, North and South, have had hundreds of years to be propagandized into believing that they were superior.

Just think about it this way; if Black and Brown had been in charge of shit for hundreds of years, and suddenly felt our grip slipping on things, then we might be willing to support/get behind a Black/Brown Trump. Maybe, instead of "Make America Great Again," the code for "Make America White Again," we would have baseball caps with "Keep America Us."

I wasn't wrapping this stuff absolutely, but I had reached the point where I felt that I could get it done with just a few more sessions with Rufus. I drove down to the shopping mall parking lot, parked and waited for Rufus to appear. No Rufus. It was late October and the political picture was red hot. Biden with an African-Indian (from India) woman? The Left exploded with joy. And a whole lot of other people on all sides of the political spectrum. Why not an African woman of Asian descent?

Trump and Pence paraded the usual lies in front of us, embroidered with elaborately fabricated bullshit, the Electoral College madness was on.

The White Republicans were the maddest of the Mad. It was becoming obvious, in late October, even with the greatest, most fraudulent efforts at voter suppression that anybody had ever seen, that El Tramposo was going to get his White ass kicked out of the White House.

The week before the Day (Nov. 3, 2020); I suddenly recalled that I hadn't seen Rufus in about two weeks. I felt kind of anxious. I wondered what was happening with him. I also needed a bit more from him to complete "Conversations".

I drove into the parking, really praying that I would see the brother in his usual spot. No Rufus. I had a sinking feeling in my gut. Maybe he's been doing his night walking number and sleeping in the day time. I drove around to the back of Mr. Kim's liquor store.

No tent. I sat there for a few minutes, trying to process this. No tent. No Rufus. Now what?

I drove back around to the parking lot, doing everything in my head to maintain my cool. I parked, put my mask on, and decided to approach the "Likka Sto' gang." I was a little surprised to see all five of the men hanging out were wearing masks. I'd never seen that before.

Five men, no women. Where was Mrs. Glover? "Molly." She would know where Rufus was. They knew me, from seeing me with Rufus. I could be pretty sure that they knew a helluva lot now about me than I knew about them.

"Hey, any of you brothers seen Mrs. Glover, Molly?" Maybe it was my imagination, but it seemed like all five heads sort of drooped at the same time.

"She caught the virus," somebody mumbled behind his mask. It didn't really matter which one had spoken. The message was clear, "Molly" was gone, dead.

"When?" That was all I could think of asking.

"Three days ago."

These guys were grieving and for them, these macho brothers, the mask was a perfect cover. I turned to walk away, stunned by the news. One last question. "Rufus?"

One of the men jerked his thumb in the direction of the liquor store. "Ask Mr. Kim."

It was only a hundred yards or so, but my legs felt stiff, wooden, like they didn't want to take me where I wanted to go. Mr. and Mrs. Kim were standing behind this elevated counter. They both looked at me as I walked in. Mr. Kim walked from behind the counter and gestured for me to follow him.

My legs felt even more wooden, following him thru the storeroom and out onto the back porch/area. He positioned himself about ten yards to my left, draped his mask around his neck, reached into his shirt pocket for his cigarettes, offered me one. I nodded no. He lit up and took a deep drag. I stared at the vacant space where Rufus once had his tent. Mr. Kim started talking, like he was talking to himself.

"I hadn't seen him for a few days, about a week. I just assumed that he was doing the 'night walking,' he used to call it." Another deep drag.

"Finally, about three days ago, my wife said, 'You should go back there and check, maybe he has had an accident or something,' Just as I was about to open the flap to his tent, he said, in a very weak voice, 'don't come in here, man, I'm sick.'

I ran back inside, called the hospital. They came right away and took him." Another deep drag.

"They listed me as the primary contact person. And this morning they called to tell me that he had died." Deep drag. Someone might've thought we were stone carvings, just standing there. I didn't know what to say. Tears were rolling slowly down Mr. Kim's cheeks.

"He was a very strong, very independent, very brave man." That was the way he ended it. That was the way he left me standing there, staring at the empty space where Rufus once lived. I don't know how long I stood there, trying to make some other kind of reality happen. I just didn't want to make myself believe that this little giant was gone, that I would never see him; that I would never have the chance to talk to him again.

Finally, God only knows how long, I staggered thru Mr. Kim's liquor store. I felt the urge to buy a fifth of something, to go home and just blot myself out. I resisted the urge because I knew, if I gave into that urge, I would be drunk for a long time.

"Willie, we pulled it off! I don't want to bore you with all of the legal details, but just let me say this — my stuff is done! You hear me?! Done! I'll be able to pull out of here the last week in November. We'll be able to spend our first Christmas together. Our first New Year. I'm so excited!

Awright, let me calm down. Heard from Sally Abrams. She is totally excited about 'Conversations'.

She'll be e-mailing you in a couple days. It looks like you might have a top of the line agency in your back pocket. Isn't that what every writer wants and needs?

Well, sweetheart, that's it for the moment. Give me a jingle when you get the time. I love you...."

I listened to ZiZi's bright, enthusiastic message about three times. I needed something to cheer me up. I sprawled on my sofa and stared up at the ceiling for about an hour. I didn't want to return her call with a lot of doom and gloom in my voice.

Finally, I pulled myself together to return her call. I was semi-praying that she wouldn't be at home, that I could leave a cheerful little message. No such luck.

"Willie, it's so good to hear your voice! I was hoping you would call. You got my message?"

"Every breathless word...."

"Is that how I sounded?"

"Yes, you did, sweetheart. And I'm so glad..."

It was like I had run out of words, what else could I say?

"I'm glad too, Willie. I miss you so much. But don't let me get off on a sentimental jag right now. I'll save it for when we're together."

"You said it would be the last week in November. That's perfect. I love the idea of starting off the New Year with you."

"Me too. Look, let's talk more about this tomorrow, I gotta run."

Busy woman, always doing something. I liked that.

"Oh, one last thing before I run – Sally Abrams called me earlier, she wanted to tell me that your fifty pages 'resonated'. That's agent speak for – she really digs the work! Talk to you tomorrow.!"

"Bye."

I sprawled back on the sofa after our conversation, satisfied that I had pulled it off, that I had made myself sound cheerful enough to disguise the pain I was feeling. I don't know where the tears came from, but they started coming and went on for a while. I couldn't really understand what it was that made me feel like crying, but I gave into it. I had a major case of duh blues.

I received Sally Abrams's email the next day.

> *"Willie West, sorry for the delay. I've shared your pages with John Hasoff and Ralph Wernick, my partners, and we're in agreement that we would like to deal with this work on your behalf. Manuscript?*
>
> *We look forward to hearing from you,*
>
> *Best, Sally Abrams"*

It all seemed to be happening too fast for me. I felt "weirded out" (as one of my dope smoking buddies used to say) by all of the stuff that just seemed to cave in on me. It was 2 a.m. in the morning before I finally figured out a reasonably honest reply to make to Sally Abrams's e-mail.

> *"Dear Ms. Abrams,*
>
> *I've received your gracious invitation to send the complete 'Conversations' manuscript. I will be sending you the manuscript, but it's going to take a few weeks before I can do that. Right now, I'm dealing with an emotional problem caused by the death of a friend and it will take a moment or two for me to make a few corrections in the manuscript before I send it.*
>
> *Sincerely,*
>
> *Willie West."*

I was a little surprised to receive a reply the next day.

> *"Dear Willie, we do understand how much emotional events can affect the creative side of our lives. Take your time, we will be here for you.*
>
> > *Sincerely yours,*
> > *Sally Abrams."*

CHAPTER 19

I didn't fall completely to pieces. I lazer beamed on the pages (starting on p. 51) that I was going to send Sally Abrams. I corrected small details, re-wrote a few events, made certain that I had the flavor of Rufus simmering in the pot.

I got all the way up to our last meeting, the place we were when we had our last meeting.

"Do you feel a little guilty, maybe responsible for her being where she is today?"

"Not really. What you have to remember, Willie, is real simple – shit happens."

I went to the beach, staggered around like a delinquent drunk, looking for the right way to bring the "Conversations" to an end. I felt like I was inside of some weird kind of maze. But, in the middle of all of my angst, I carefully checked my ballot and sent it in. No more Trump.

ZiZi kept me up to date on the "beast monster's" tricks and antics. Biden was the winner.

"Willie, I don't know what it's like down there, in Long Beach, but San Francisco is in the freak out zone. People are dancing in the streets, with and without masks. Music is playing everywhere and the plague is killing people left and right. I want to be in your arms so bad ...."

I felt the jubilation too. It wasn't as exalted for me as it was for her, but I felt the tension grow slack. I think it was best expressed on the face of a *Whatever Card* I saw in Renee's "Shades of Africa". A beautiful little cocoa colored boy's face peeks around the corner of a thatched hut and asks' -- "Is the Trickster gone yet?"

Of course, losing the election wasn't enough for the Trickster; he had to keep on losing and losing and losing, in the courts, the re-counts, everywhere. He even lost an attempted coup, using thirteen weirdass White Republicans as a suicide squad. He was still losing when ZiZi made her way into my arms.

[When a fiend like the beast monster lost his Twitter account, you knew his world was gone, well, almost.]

ZiZi Lago (soon to be Mrs. West) came to me, to my large roomed, one-bedroom third floor apartment on Linden Avenue, at 8:30 pm, November 27th, 2020. We stood in the front room and held onto each other for at least ten minutes.

We had visited each other, but this was different. Ceremonies were going to be performed, we knew that. But for Now, for our time with each other, we just felt the urge to hold each other. I have to smile, thinking back on our first moments together.

I opened the champagne; we curled up on the sofa, sipped our bubbly and talked 'til dawn. One of the most important things we talked about was the house we were going to live in.

"I think I may have found our spot, but you'll have to check it out."

There was this house on Olive Avenue, between Myrtle on the east and Atlantic on the west. I had made it my business to drive past this house in the middle of the block for a full week, at different times of the day and night. I wanted to make sure it wasn't a noisy, drug ridden scene. It wasn't.

[I'll save the story of how ZiZi Lago-West out maneuvered three other couples to get into our house.]

["Willie, we're going to have this house, this is the one."]

Re-tracing a bit. We were almost four days inside of our blissful bubble before reality reared its ugly head.

"What's with Rufus?"

We were sitting at the kitchen table, spooning up blueberry/banana smoothies at midnight when the question popped up. I hated to tell her that Rufus was dead, another victim of the virus/plague. I don't think I've ever heard such an anguished sound in my whole life when she moaned – "O my God, no! no! no!"

We left the table and went into the bedroom, to do a really hard moment that lasted for a couple hours. I had to make a confession.

"ZiZi, I don't think I have the classic so called 'Writer's Block.' It's just that I feel, I want to be true to Rufus's spirit, as wacky as that might sound."

We nodded off, cuddled in each other's arms, feeling sad.

The delicious aroma of freshly brewing coffee woke me up. ZiZi brought a cup into the bedroom, on a tray, all spiffed up in a black jogging suit. This was looking good, real good.

"Where do you jog?"

"Let me drink this and I'll show you." Our married life was beginning. We drove over to Bixby Park and, Lawd H'mercy, found a parking space.

"Oh, I remember this."

We trotted down the hill, passing the huge yoga class on the bluff overlooking the ocean. We smiled to each other at the sight of all the butts sticking up in the air. Down to the beach, for a jog to the last lifeguard stand. And back.

I was sweating like a pig and was completely out of gas at the end of our jog.

"Looks like I'm going to have to up my game to jog with you, sweet thang."

She just nodded in agreement and grabbed me around the shoulders.

"I love you, Willie, I wouldn't care if you couldn't run at all."

A man likes to hear things like that. Back to the pad for hot showers and a midday nap. Something I hadn't had in a long time. I could feel her eyes on me before I was fully awake.

"ZiZi, what're you doing, baby?"

"Just watching you sleep."

We shared a smile and a gentle kiss and then she squirmed up against my right side.

"Willie, I've been thinking about something you said – concerning being true to Rufus's spirit. Now, please don't get me wrong. You're the writer in the family.

I'm hell on a brief, but not so hot on creative writing...."

I gave her a little peck on the nose and lips to grant her permission to give me her thoughts.

"Well, you're writing about a person who was obviously very creative, why shouldn't you be creative with him at the end? I mean, does he really have to die the way he died? Couldn't you have something else happen? What else did he want to do in his life? The same thing with this lady you've spoken about."

"Mrs. Annette Glover, 'Molly'."

"Yeah, what else was she going to do with her life, other than drink herself to death?"

I was crawling out of bed, struggling to put on my bathrobe and get to my desk at the same time. ZiZi had lit the fire.

※

It took me approximately three hot days to do what I had to do with Rufus. Just as he said, he wanted to go back to Australia, to his wife Yvonne and his sons, Melvin and Ervin. No matter whether they existed or not.

I slipped Mr. Kim into the action to make it real. Fantasy is the Mother of all creations.

※

"Yo Willie writer man, I'm gone. I've been trying to get back to the Enchanted Land, my Australia, for years. I will be in touch with you, don't worry about that. But I had to hat up. Give my best regards to your Lady ZiZi.

Bright Moments
Melvin Montaigne Dixon III
a.k.a. 'Likka Sto' Rufus"

I stood at Mr. Kim's elevated counter, staring at the note he had just given me.

"Please step to the side, please."

Of course, he had customers to serve. I moved to one side. He sold the brothers their favorite pints of booze and re-directed his attention back to me.

"Rufus gave me this note for you about two weeks ago; I've been waiting for you to come in."

"He says he is going back to Australia in the note. How could he go back to Australia?

Where did he get the money?"

Mr. Kim leaned across the counter to whisper, "He won some lottery money."

"How much?"

"I can't tell you that."

"Well, just give me a ball park figure. Was it more than ten grand?"

He nodded yes.

"But less than twenty grand?"

Once again, he nodded yes.

I got a pint of Seagram's gin to go with my ginger beer. I was going home to write a beautiful ending to "Conversations with Rufus" and celebrate his good fortune. Mr. Kim leaned over to whisper to me again as I was leaving.

"Please don't speak about this to anyone; I don't want people to overrun my store. O.k.?"

Mrs. Annette Glover's story was much easier to deal with. After years of being under the influence of the demon wine, she had stumbled across Sylvia Browne's book, "The Other Side and Back." Sylvia Browne, the psychic woman, had given her the experiences she needed to straighten her life out.

The psychic's words had jolted her soul, returned her mind to the thoughts of the beautiful life she remembered as a devout Christian. It wasn't easy for her to have a Rebirth, but she pulled it off with the help of a vibrant preacher named Warnock.

Maybe I could say – "The rest is history." But who knows?

❦

Like I said earlier, ZiZi danced circles around these couples who were trying to get our house. I almost felt sorry for them, our competitors.

"Willie, remember what I said, we're going to have this house, this is the one."

"Never will forget it. So, how did you pull it off?"

"No, baby, how did we pull it off? It had to do with concentration and focus. Most people are not focused or concentrated. That's what gives us an advantage over most people. I'm not being egotistical, or anything like that. You're focused on your writing and I'm focused on the law. Dig it?"

The house was built way back when, but it was our house, a "work in progress"; but it was <u>our</u> house, not an apartment with heavy footed folks above and crazy music lovers underneath. Aside from everything else, we were lovers in love with our love. Our love was strong enough to see the "Beast monster thing" (ZiZi added nicknames faster than I could keep track) as though he was a creature in the rear-view mirror.

As Rufus once said – "Shit happens."

ZiZi practically forced Cockrand and Associates to establish a Civil Rights Div. in their law firm (five wizard lawyers under her) after the January 6th invasion of the White House, as a firm condition of her coming aboard.

There was no opposition. Mr. Cockrand spoke volumes in an e-mail, when he informed ZiZi – "*We are first and foremost, attorneys for the rule of law. And I am an African-American citizen of this Democracy. Proceed!*"

That's what the man said. And from that point onward, it was On! ZiZi's Civil Rights Div. had a bunch of cases to deal with, both cold and hot. Seems that the police couldn't stop shooting People to death, 'specially People of Color.

Despite the fact that we were doing well financially, in the middle of the plague, we had decided not to have any babies until the Trumpesto Madness had calmed down a bit.

❦

"Can you get ready for this?! This dirty rotten snake dog asshole cop is trying to make us believe that he shot, six times, and killed this sister 'because she was reaching into her waistband for a weapon, and he feared for his life.' The sister was nine months pregnant and didn't have a weapon. We have lots of work to do!"

ZiZi's Civil Rights Div. at Cockrands (those five attorneys) were busy as usual. The Abrams-Hasoff-Wernick Agency made a very lucrative sale of "Conversations", alerting a couple foxy producers to the scent of new blood. Nothing like a new movie.

And Sally Abrams is enthusiastic about my latest bio-novel, dedicated to the memory of Melvin Montaigne Dixon III, a.k.a. Likka Sto' Rufus. The prophetic title is **"Shit Happens"**.

Printed in the United States
by Baker & Taylor Publisher Services